'That sounded l

'A threat?' Rick turn
the fading light mean
a harshly defined and

'About seeing a lot of us.' Thank goodness for
the darkness, which meant that her own
giveaway rise of colour went unnoticed.

'No, Elizabeth, not a threat. I've never yet
threatened a woman, and I don't intend to start
now. Look on it more as a promise!'

Dear Reader

The first few months of a new year are a time for looking forward and wondering what the future holds for us. There are no such worries when you pick up a Mills & Boon story, though—you're guaranteed to find an exciting, heart-warming romance! This month, as usual, we've got some real treats in store for you. So, whatever 1995 brings you, you can be sure of one thing: if you're reading Mills & Boon, it's going to be a year of romance!

The Editor

Sharon Kendrick was born in West London. Leaving school at sixteen to try a variety of jobs and see the world, Sharon then trained as a nurse. In the best romantic tradition, she fell in love with and married a doctor. While expecting her second child, Sharon got down to writing her first romantic novel. She loves writing, and the fact that such enjoyable work fits in so well with her life.

Recent titles by the same author:

SWEET MADNESS

POTENT
AS POISON

BY
SHARON KENDRICK

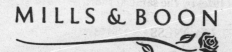

MILLS & BOON LIMITED
ETON HOUSE, 18-24 PARADISE ROAD
RICHMOND, SURREY TW9 1SR

To the ice-dance Queen—Heather Staps
and her soppy husband, Paul!

*MILLS & BOON and the Rose Device
are trademarks of the publisher.*

*First published in Great Britain 1995
by Mills & Boon Limited*

© Sharon Kendrick 1995

*Australian copyright 1995   Philippine copyright 1995
This edition 1995*

ISBN 0 263 78897 0

*Set in Times Roman 10 on 12 pt
01-9503-49714 C*

Made and printed in Great Britain

CHAPTER ONE

'WILL there be anything else, Mrs Carson?'

At the sound of her secretary's voice Elizabeth turned from the window where she had been standing day-dreaming, lost to the world. She was tired, so tired she could have sat back in her chair, perched her long, stockinged legs on the desk, and sneaked forty winks! But such laid-back behaviour wouldn't have augured well for her image as a super-bright, super-sharp company accountant, and besides, she had an appointment in— she glanced down at her watch—ten minutes' time.

'I can't think of anything else, thanks, Jenny.'

'Your voice still sounds awful—I've got another packet of throat pastilles in my desk if you want them.'

Elizabeth pushed her large tinted glasses back up her nose and smiled at the motherly-looking secretary who had been with her since the day she'd started at Meredith & Associates. 'Any more pastilles and I'll start to look like one!' she joked. 'Just show Mr Masterton straight in when he arrives, will you, then you can go?'

Jenny shook her head. 'I don't mind sticking around. To be honest, I wouldn't mind seeing if the man matches the movie-star voice!'

Elizabeth cleared her throat with the dry cough which was the legacy of last week's bout of flu, and laughed. 'Hardly! This is real life, remember? Just leave me his file, would you, Jenny? Thanks.'

Elizabeth watched as Jenny retreated and closed the office door behind her, and then she picked up the résumé on Rick Masterton.

Unusual that Jenny should have been so impressed by a client, thought Elizabeth, although as she scanned the closely typewritten pages she tended to agree with her—for who in their right mind could fail to be impressed by what read like a composite of a *Boys' Own* hero?

Her lips curved into a wry smile as she re-read the file.

Rick Masterton, aged thirty-four. Born Boston. Educated Exeter and Harvard, first class honours in law. Picked for USA Olympic skiing team, but unable to take up place due to injury to fist obtained from performing a citizen's arrest on a mugger in New York City.

Here Elizabeth smiled again, because whoever had compiled the report on Rick Masterton had written in the margin, 'This guy cannot be for *real*!'

No, indeed, thought Elizabeth, as she briefly perused the rest of the report, noting the awards, the merits, the reputation, even—and here she shook her head a little in mild disbelief—even a *philanthropist* at such a relatively tender age. No less than the wing of a children's hospital donated by him. No, she had to agree with the author of the report—he could *not* be for real!

There would have to be something wrong with him, and Elizabeth amused herself with imagining just *what*. He might be short, with a short man's insecurities. Or fat. He could—and here she shook her head—be *both*. But skiers in Olympic teams tended to have a sleek physique, not be roly-polys. She would have to wait and see for herself whether Jenny was to be disappointed.

She glanced at the discreetly expensive timepiece which gleamed on her slim wrist. Ten minutes before he was due to arrive, and she would wager that he would be punctual, as all busy and powerful men always seemed to be. Not for them the reputation-damaging mismanagement of time; not in her experience, anyhow.

She'd better go and freshen up before he arrived.

She walked into her ultra-luxurious washroom. Ridiculously luxurious, she thought, as she gazed at the sumptuous fittings, remembering how she had protested to her boss about such preferential treatment. In vain. For in Paul Meredith's eyes she was the greatest thing since sliced bread. He had shaken his blond head energetically. 'Elizabeth, you got the washroom—you keep it! You're the best and, what's more—you *deserve* the best.'

Thus she had her own private bathroom. And the amazing thing was that none of her colleagues in Paul's accountancy firm seemed to object. Elizabeth suspected that this was because she was the only woman accountant among a large band of men, and from the outset she seemed to have inspired a collective protection from them all. Which was sweet. She sighed. And uncomplicated. Just the way she wanted it. And, according to the male colleagues—and that included Paul—who had tried, and failed, to take the working relationship into more personal realms—she apparently gave off very strong vibes which said quite clearly 'don't touch'. She certainly didn't give them off consciously, though she was pleased enough for the men treating her as they would a sister, for Elizabeth had decided some years ago that her busy life of full-time work and bringing up a young son simply held no room for the complications of a relationship, particularly when all relationships seemed to fall short of the one which had changed her life forever...

She stared back at her reflection. She had grown used to her sleek grown-up working-woman look, but sometimes, just sometimes, she found it hard to believe that the calm, pristine young woman who stared back at her really was Elizabeth Carson. The linen suit was crisp and pale; very tailored and very neat, the long jacket chosen cleverly to disguise the over-lushness of her breasts. There had been too many instances in the early days of men's eyes straying to below her neck to linger there.

The cool image was deliberate, the mask she hid behind; the smart tailored clothes her shield. The metamorphosis of Elizabeth Carson. When had that insecure little orphan become this cool-looking female? It had not happened overnight, that was for sure, she thought, then bit her lip. No, not overnight. But maybe over a weekend...

She heard a light tap, and the click of the door in her office, Jenny's voice calling her name, which meant that the client was here; and she quickly turned on her heel and went out to meet him. She walked forward on the high heels she often wore which had the effect of making her already long legs appear endless, angry with herself for her daydreaming, because it was surely a disadvantage for a prospective client to find his accountant just leaving the bathroom.

But then her footsteps faltered as she saw him, heard Jenny say briskly, 'Mr Masterton for you, Mrs Carson.'

But Elizabeth scarcely registered the words as she stared at the man who seemed to fill her office. He wasn't short, or fat, or bald, she thought with something approaching hysteria. Something had happened to her vision—it was as though she was viewing him from the wrong end of a telescope. Her world had gone silent, the faint rushing of blood to every pulse-point in her body the only sound. A world that had suddenly turned upside down; her worst nightmare and her favourite dream come true. It was him.

Or had she gone insane? She forced a breath back into her lungs. Was she simply hallucinating up a fantasy? A man dreamt about and agonised over every single day for almost nine years? She had recently recovered from a bad bout of flu, and didn't the body make the mind play cruel tricks sometimes?

She blinked several times behind her glasses, and when her eyes reopened properly she saw that it was no hallucination, but indeed the nightmare, or the dream. He was here. In her office. Riccardo. The father of her son.

Dimly, through her confusion, she realised how bizarre she must look, but there was nothing she could do about it; she was literally struck speechless as hope stirred within her.

He's come back for me, she thought foolishly, her body seeming to be drawn towards his, towards the enticing warmth she remembered so well.

But as he gazed back at her, that shatteringly handsome face registering nothing but cool and faintly bored indifference, her heart plummeted as she realised that the unthinkable had happened...

He didn't recognise her!

She continued to stand, staring at him mutely, completely at a loss as to what to say or do next, forgetting that she stood in her own office with her secretary staring at her in amazement. But she could have been anywhere; all she saw was him.

He turned to Jenny. 'Is she always like this?' he mocked. 'Do you have a physician on standby?'

But before Jenny could answer, Elizabeth realised that she was going to have to pull herself together, and quickly. He had not, as she had stupidly imagined in one brief moment of madness, come back for her. Indeed, the man she had spent all those years yearning for had absolutely no idea who she was. And what had she expected? For there had been nothing in his treatment of her at the time to indicate that she was anything more than one of a long line of young women he had enticed into his bed...

And this bitter realisation flooded her like poison, removing all her remaining fantasies and replacing them with a steely anger. 'Mr Masterton,' she acknowledged coolly. 'How nice to meet you.' But her words rang with the hollowness of insincerity, and she didn't offer him her hand. She saw his eyes briefly glitter, then harden. They stood facing each other across the desk, like two boxers about to commence a fight, and Elizabeth forced herself to think clearly—there had to be a diplomatic way of doing what she was about to do.

She gave a poor imitation of a smile, forcing her voice not to betray a modicum of the desperation she was feeling. 'Won't you sit down, Mr Masterton?'

A muscle stirred in the depths of an olive cheek. Clearly irritated, he gave a small shake of his head, and she realised that if he *had* sat down she would have had the psychological advantage of towering over him, whereas now, even with her spiky high heels on, he most definitely towered over *her*. She was going to have to get out of here, even for a few moments, but professional courtesy demanded that she offer him some form of refreshment, at least.

'Might I offer you some coffee?' But the words sounded as though they were choking her.

Unmoving, he continued to subject her to that narrow-eyed irritation. 'Thank you,' he said, with sarcastic emphasis. 'But no.'

'Then in that case—Jenny.' She gave something approaching a smile to the woman who stood in front of her, aware of the look of puzzlement in her eyes. 'You've worked for long enough. I can manage here on my own now. I'll see you in the morning.'

'Yes, Mrs Carson.'

Even Jenny's professionalism couldn't keep the trace of bewilderment out of her voice, thought Elizabeth—and who could blame her, with her boss behaving as though she'd had a complete brainstorm? Elizabeth saw a sardonic dark eyebrow raised in Jenny's direction and she could have hugged her secretary for very pointedly ignoring it.

As Jenny walked out and the office door closed behind her, Elizabeth met the cool gaze head-on. 'If you'll just excuse me for a moment—I'd like a few moments to straighten myself out.'

He didn't reply; he didn't have to—the expression on his face said it all. Strange woman.

She managed to make her way into the washroom without stumbling, turning the tap on full blast as if hoping that the running water would wash everything away, leaving her the same woman as five minutes ago with no problems other than of a practical nature; problems she could deal with quite easily.

Quickly, she ran the pulse-points of her wrists under the cool water in an effort to slow the thundering of her pulses which had caused two high spots of scarlet to flush over her cheekbones, so that they stood out in startling contrast to the drained whiteness of her face. She had to stay in control. Not cowering out here. In control.

And wasn't she over-reacting like crazy? It was obviously coincidence that had brought him here today. Just because he had forgotten that once, a lifetime ago... And here she bit her lip.

Once, he had slept with her.

Which meant nothing. Not these days. Not to a man like that. That she at the time had chosen to misinterpret what was obviously just meant to be a very enjoyable yet simply casual dalliance was down to her, not him. And she had no right whatsoever to burden him with the repercussions of that fateful weekend.

He was a prospective client, nothing more. But already she knew for certain that she didn't want him as a client. She had loved him, for God's sake—there was no way she could work for him as if nothing had ever happened. And she imagined that, after what had just occurred, the feeling would be mutual. And yet, as she turned to go back into her office, some protesting voice in her head shouted, Tell him! Tell him about Peter.

He was still standing, and had his back to her, looking out of her window, but as the washroom door closed behind Elizabeth, he turned.

Tell him? she thought, but the wavering only lasted for a second as their eyes met. He really *doesn't* recognise me, she thought, and an immense sadness washed over her as the last remnant of her girlish dreams crumbled and died. 'Won't you take a seat?' She indicated the chair before her desk with a long, elegant hand.

He paused no longer than a second, before lowering his long-legged frame into the chair opposite her own. 'Thank you.' But the courtesy belied the tone of his voice; that spoke nothing but derision.

He waited until she herself had sat down, watching her closely, so closely that at any moment she expected him to say, 'Beth!' but of course he didn't, and when he did speak his words were anything but friendly.

'Are you normally so hostile towards prospective clients, Mrs Carson?' he said coldly.

Something of her normal unflappability began to gain ascendancy. 'I've been under a lot of pressure recently,' she said. 'And this wasn't helped by a bad bout of flu from which I'm only just recovering,' she returned calmly, but it fell far short of an apology and what was more, they both knew it.

She couldn't miss the imperceptible knitting together of the dark brows, the flash of fire in the blue-green eyes as he acknowledged her rudeness.

But she had *intended* to be insulting. Recklessly, she neither thought nor cared about the consequences—she wanted him *out* of here, and quickly. Because somehow, quite without knowing it, he was playing havoc with her equilibrium. Why else would the palms of her hands be so sticky that she was having to surreptitiously use her skirt to soak up their dampness, or her heart be hammering so furiously that she feared for her health? He had turned her world upside down once before, and she would do everything in her power to make sure that he didn't do so a second time.

The spectacular blue-green eyes continued to glitter as he registered her pugnacious expression, and she expected a snapped retort, but she was wrong, for he leaned back in the chair as if he had all the right in the world to be there.

'Have a problem with men, do you, honey?' He stared suggestively at her short, almost boyish haircut, and she caught his drift immediately, a dull brick-red colour flaring over her cheeks.

'Just what are you getting at?'

He shrugged broad, broad shoulders. 'I'm a liberated man—I can take it. You know what they say: "different strokes for different folks".'

'If you're suggesting what I *think* you're suggesting,' she spluttered furiously, 'then I can assure you I'm not!'

'Well, that's something,' he said, in a soft, almost dangerous voice. 'Because let me tell you, Mrs Carson— I've heard a good deal about your particular *talents*.'

Did his eyes briefly flick from lips to breast—the slight flare of the aristocratic nostrils an outward sign that he had responded to her physically? Or was her imagination running riot? I have to get him out of here, she thought weakly.

'Mr Masterton!' She could stand no more. Tension crackled in the air, like the first light to a bonfire. 'I think it's better if you leave now, don't you?'

'Leave?' His tone was mocking, but his eyes were as hard as diamonds. 'But I've only just arrived.'

Oh, those eyes. Blue-green, the colour of a sunwashed sea; how they dazzled as they mocked.

'I'm sorry.' Patently, she wasn't. 'But it's obvious that we aren't going to be able to work with each other.' She pushed together an already tidy sheaf of papers in a gesture she intended to be dismissive, but to her despair he leaned even further back in the chair.

'Oh?' he queried. 'And why's that?'

She found herself wanting to shout at him, because his presence was somehow making her mind flare up with disturbing images as she found herself remembering his kiss, the exquisite perfection of his lovemaking. She found herself remembering his dark head flung back, a look of pure ecstasy on his face, caught up in the same heart-stopping release that she'd discovered with him... For a moment she hovered on the brink of tears, but with gritty determination they were gone before there was even the hint of a shimmer in her eyes.

She drew a deep breath, managed a calm voice, even a rueful half-smile to play on her lips. She did her 'we're all adults here' approach. 'Come on, Mr Masterton—let's not be naïve. We haven't exactly—hit it off, have we? A personality clash—whatever you like to call it. It happens.'

The eyes narrowed, and Elizabeth had the uncanny feeling that he had seen through her little show of pretence and witnessed the discomfiture which lay beneath. She also got the feeling that rejection was something he neither knew nor liked. 'On the contrary,' he said, in the deep American drawl. 'There's nothing more invigorating than a little *conflict*. It sharpens the mind and——' his eyes glimmered '—makes such a refreshing change.'

He had leaned back in his chair, and now she was *sure* that his eyes had briefly travelled up the pale, silk-stockinged length of her legs, just visible beneath her desk. She despised herself for the tremor which trembled through her slender body like a feather caught on the wind. Even worse, she saw the corner of his mouth lift as he acknowledged it without surprise.

He had, she decided sadly, lost nothing of the almost tangible sex-appeal which had swept her off her feet as an eighteen-year-old. There was not a sound in the room as they stared at one another, puzzled interest in his eyes as the tension grew.

The years had been kind to him, thought Elizabeth. Very kind. She knew from his file that he was thirty-four now, and he carried himself with all the authority of a rich and powerful man.

His looks were unique—she had never seen another man like him. Perhaps it was the combination of those amazingly light eyes, so at odds when fringed by lashes and brows of the same deep ebony as his hair. Eyes so light that they looked startlingly luminous, set in the pale olive complexion which she recalled him telling her he owed to an Italian mother. The nose, naturally enough,

was Roman—curved and carved into a haughtily aristocratic profile. And yet the body, and the accent—they
were all-American. Solid, honed muscular perfection,
with a deep, drawling movie-star voice. He was—he
always had been—one hell of a package.

She leaned forward. 'Listen to me. I can't work for
you. I can recommend other accountants——'

'No.' The voice was quietly decisive. 'I want *you* to
look after my business.'

She had never done anything like this in her life, not
risked her job by refusing to take on such a valuable
client. She prayed that Paul would never find just why
she was doing it. 'I don't think you understand——'

'No, Mrs Carson,' he interrupted, and his voice rang
out in the tone of a man who was used to calling the
shots. 'I don't think that *you* understand. I was given
your name because you happen to have a specialty—you
handle the accounts of law firms, and that's my line of
business. I was told that you are the best, and that's why
I want you to represent me. I feel I should warn
you——' and here his gaze was mocking '—that I always
get what I want.'

I know you do, she thought. She had one last try. 'Mr
Masterton, let me recommend you the names of some
other accountancy firms.'

He leaned towards her, so that their faces were mere
inches away from each other. 'But I want *this* accountancy firm, Mrs Carson. And, more importantly—
I want *you*. I don't *care* if you don't like me—for
whatever reason. Your hang-ups about men are of no
concern to me. I'm asking you to keep my books, not
marry me.'

Elizabeth blanched at the unwitting irony of his words.

His eyes were piercing her with that blue-green light. 'I have legal contacts and friends in England who have used you and been extremely pleased with the work you've put in. What they failed to mention was that you seem to have some problem with communication skills. Not that that matters—an accountant needs to be good with figures, not words.' The slanting eyes narrowed still further. 'What I *do* find intriguing, though, is your obvious reluctance to have my account. Tell me, is Paul Meredith aware that one of his senior accountants does her best to turn away lucrative offers of work?'

She heard the underlying threat spoken with silky menace, and it drew her up short, so that she started as she realised that she was in danger of jeopardising the career she had worked so hard for. Here was a man used to getting what he wanted, after all—and she suddenly recognised that a man like this, to whom everything in life had come so easily, would look on her reluctance to be hired by him as some kind of challenge. Why not just surrender gracefully to the inevitable? She looked at him steadily. 'Very well,' she said. 'You, as the client, obviously know best, and I shall of course endeavour to do my best for you.'

'Oh, for sure,' he agreed softly, and then his eyes narrowed in intense concentration, just for a second, as if something was puzzling him. Elizabeth held her breath, certain again that he was about to remember her, but the moment passed.

She cleared her throat, pulling a portfolio towards her, and, picking up her fountain pen with a hand which was, amazingly, quite steady, she looked up at him expectantly.

'Mr Masterton——'

'Rick.'

She wondered briefly why he now used the American diminutive of his Italian name before shaking her head. 'That may be the American way, but I'm afraid it's not ours. If you don't mind, I'd prefer to keep things on a formal footing.'

But he obviously did mind, because as he looked at her, that perfect mouth twisted with derision. 'God, but you're uptight,' he observed.

Pen poised, she looked at him as politely as if he had not just insulted her. 'Shall we get on?' she enquired frostily, and she saw him give a terse if somewhat reluctant nod. 'Now then, about your business. What kind of business do you intend setting up?'

'Why, a law firm, of course,' he stated. 'What else?'

'But you qualified in the States. And as an American barrister——'

'Attorney,' he corrected.

'Attorney, then. Surely you aren't allowed to practise over here without taking extra exams?'

'I'm not planning to. I'm leaving that to some very able English colleagues. I'm just here to set it all up. As soon as the chambers are established, then I'm back off to the States.'

She couldn't keep the relief from her voice. 'That means that you're only here temporarily?'

His mouth twisted. 'Yes, Mrs Carson. A few months at most.'

Thank God. 'And do you intend for your law firm to be general—I mean tackling company law, fraud, divorce...?'

He gave an almost imperceptible nod of the head as if acknowledging that now—at least—she was beginning to speak some sense! 'Oh, no, Mrs Carson. Like you, I have a specialty.'

She got the strangest feeling of foreboding. 'Which is?'

'In America we call it "palimony". I specialise in establishing the nature of common-law relationships, and negotiating a corresponding financial settlement. That's one thing I do. My main interest, though, lies in the welfare of children.'

Some protective instinct deep within her stirred, powerful enough to keep her face poker blank. 'Children?' she echoed.

'Yes, indeed. You see—I specialise in child custody cases.'

With an effort, Elizabeth only just prevented her mouth from falling open in sheer, disbelieving horror. 'Child custody cases?' she queried, and for one wild moment terror invaded her. *He knows*, she thought desperately. He wants Peter.

'Sure.' He shrugged big, powerful shoulders. 'I've represented a lot of fathers contesting cases in the States. We've managed to break a lot of new ground.'

She swallowed, twirling the gold pen between her fingers like a drum majorette, so he wouldn't see that her hands were shaking. 'Oh? How's that?' She saw his big frame relax as he warmed to the subject.

'Society's changing. Women no longer have the right to assume that they are the child's best custodian.'

Elizabeth felt slightly sick, her vision a little blurred, and her hand reached up so that she could rub her finger inside the rim of her shirt collar, the cool air to her neck making her vision thankfully clear again. 'But a mother surely has a much stronger right than the man,' she argued, her voice a hoarse whisper. 'A *biological* right— given to them by nature, by the fact that they were the one who carried the child, gave birth to it, cared for it——'

He stared at her. 'Nature over nurture?' he queried. 'But nature is often indiscriminate, is it not? A child's future shouldn't be governed by something as haphazard as the laws of nature.'

'So you discriminate *against* women, do you, Mr Masterton? Use your trained lawyer's silver tongue to buy your rich clients their child's future?'

He frowned, as if momentarily puzzled by the reappearance of her aggressive stance. 'On the contrary— I judge each case on its particular merits, and I pride myself on acting in the *child's* best interests. But for too long fathers have suffered bad deals meted out to them by sentimental judges—giving them limited access which is laughable. At the very least there should be joint custody; unlimited access.' He seemed to take in her unsmiling mouth. The dark eyes flicked to her left hand.

'Are you married?' he queried. 'You are a Mrs, and yet you don't wear a ring. Your husband must be a very liberated man.'

'I—*was* married,' she said slowly, the normal evasion she used when speaking of her past automatically shaping her answer.

'Ah! No doubt why you speak with such fervour on the subject of child custody.'

He had assumed, as most people tended to, that her marriage had ended through divorce, rather than death.

His eyes narrowed with interest as he continued. 'A fervour which goes against that very——' and the eyes flicked now to the severe lines of her suit '—cool exterior.' He smiled at her, a smile which could conquer all. 'I trust I haven't opened up any old wounds. Do you have children, Mrs Carson?'

She put her pen down on top of the folder, and gave him a chilly smile. The chilliest in her repertoire. 'Mr Masterton,' she said, her slightly condescending manner not lost on him, 'fascinating as I'm sure you find it, my personal life really has nothing to do with why you're here, does it? So perhaps if we could turn to a few salient points about the size of your prospective law firm...?'

He didn't like that, she realised. Not at all. He was not a man women would usually put down like that, not unless they had been hurt by him, of course—and he was ignorant of the fact that she belonged to that no doubt large band of women who *had* been hurt by him. And he must, she decided, that fiercely protective instinct coming to the fore once more—he must *remain* ignorant of the fact. For Peter's sake.

She asked her questions, and he answered them, but there was an underlying tension which crackled in the air like electricity for the rest of the interview, and she saw that brief look of puzzlement cross his face once again.

You must make an effort, a voice urged silently. Stop antagonising him—for she recognised that he could be a dangerous adversary if aroused. He's your client, the voice insisted, so drop the spiky manner. Ooze charm and he'll probably run a mile. But she also knew that she wasn't going to be able to keep up this dangerous farce for much longer.

She straightened the pile of papers on her desk, and looked at him expectantly—a polite if somewhat prim smile on her lips. 'Well, Mr Masterton——' And with an effort she increased the wattage of the smile. 'That all seems to be fairly conclusive—I'll have my secretary type up details for you first thing.' And she need hardly meet with him again after today, thank God. Most of their communication would be by letter, maybe the occasional phone call.

Her words were intended as the precursor to a conclusion of the meeting. He knew it and she knew it, but he remained unmoving. Watchful, yet relaxed—a man totally at ease with the world, and his highly privileged place in it. She could see his forehead creased in concentration, as if he was trying to work out something in his head. Was he sensitive enough to have picked up anything from her behaviour?

In an effort to distract him, she spoke again. 'Was there anything else you wanted, Mr Masterton? Anything you wanted to ask me?'

'Yes.'

His next words filled her with both elation and horror.

'Have dinner with me tonight.'

The laugh she gave was hoarse, and her voice cracked with the effort of it. The irony was not lost on her. For years she would have given everything she owned for just such an invitation, but now, in view of what he'd just said on the subject of custody—the reality of it was far too threatening even to contemplate. She put her hand over her breastbone. 'Dinner?'

Still watching her closely, he smiled. But it was a cold smile, a smile which stayed light years away from his eyes. 'Don't look so shocked,' he murmured. 'Surely a man has asked you out to dinner before? You've been married too, so why sit there, your hand over your heart, as if I've suggested something which is in some way indecent?'

She gave him a chilly smile. 'You're a client,' she pointed out.

He shrugged. 'Nothing in the rule book to say we can't eat together. Let's call it a business dinner.'

'But I thought we'd discussed everything we ought to— so how can it be?'

The dark-featured face remained disturbingly enigmatic. 'You're quite right of course, Mrs Carson. I'd like to have dinner with you because you intrigue me.'

She stood up, her heart beating like a piston. 'Oh?'

'Mmm. You do. Very much.' He stood up also. 'Your manner towards me has been remarkable, to say the least. Your secretary was taken aback, too—so you're obviously acting out of character. When people behave out of character there's always a reason. And I wonder why. Is it me?'

'You mean you're amazed that I haven't responded to your abundant charm?' she said angrily.

The eyes narrowed, and he smiled. 'I haven't used it yet,' he murmured. 'Do you want me to?'

She could have kicked herself. 'I want you to let me get off home now,' she said baldly. She badly needed to get him out of here, before she did or said something which would have dire repercussions for both her, and Peter.

'Sure.' He glanced at his watch on his wrist. 'It's getting late. Do you have a date?'

The perfect solution! 'I—yes. Yes I do.'

'Then I'll see you to the lift,' he said smoothly.

Helpless, trapped—for she how could she pretend her eagerness to be away and then linger around the office?— she reluctantly picked up her briefcase. 'Thank you.'

The carpeted walk to the executive lift seemed like miles, the silence which hung in the air between them not an easy one, yet he, at least, showed no desire to break it, while she could think of nothing neutral to say. He stood aside to let her into the lift first, and she saw, to her horror, that he intended to accompany her! Alone, in the tiny confines of a lift—where even with people you knew well the atmosphere was always strained as you all stared mutely at the flashing lights. But alone with Riccardo—she corrected herself—alone with Rick Masterton...

The lift doors slid open, and she went in first, putting her hand out immediately to press 'ground' with one plain, unvarnished fingernail, but he had beaten her to it, his finger firmly on the 'hold' button as he stared down at her, his face shadowed so that the light eyes appeared darkly fathomless as they searched her face as if in pursuit of the answer to a question which only she knew.

She shivered; nerves, fear and excitement—yes, excitement—combined to make her slender body tremble. For no matter how much her logical mind told her that after everything that had happened she should no longer be affected in any way by this man, her body knew differently. Her body betrayed her, as it had betrayed her so long ago. Her reaction to this man had always been disturbingly unique, and some things, it seemed, never changed.

Mute, and mere feet away from him, she saw the sharp planes and angles of that ruggedly handsome face, and some soft yearning deep at the very heart of her cried out its request. *Tell him*, said the voice. This is the man you once loved—so tell him about his son. Tell him about Peter. And she trembled again. But then she saw him give a tiny nod of his head, as though her helpless tremble in response to his proximity was merely par for the course.

'The signals you're sending out are delightfully and intriguingly mixed,' he murmured. 'You seem unable to quite decide whether to tell me to go to hell or to give in to what you *really* want to do...'

She saw the predatory light firing in the depths of those incredible eyes and she thought that he was moving towards her as though to kiss her. My God—he *was*! And if he kissed her...

She stepped back. His hand had left the 'hold' button, and she took the opportunity to press for the ground floor—and the lift purred into action.

She expected irritation on his part but there was none. Instead nothing but a kind of wry amusement, as though he were enjoying the silent tussle.

'You like to fence, then?' he queried. 'That's good. Because so do I.'

'Evasive action was obviously called for,' she said coldly.

He laughed. 'Pity.'

'Tell me,' she enquired cuttingly, 'do you always foist your attentions on perfect strangers?'

But he didn't look at all offended as he shook his head. 'That's the peculiar thing,' he murmured. 'I don't.'

And all of a sudden the game they were playing utterly sickened her. Here she was, almost flirting with a man who could, she realised—take away everything that she held dear.

The lift doors opened, and the commissionaire stepped forward.

'Night, Mrs Carson,' he said cheerfully. 'Afraid you've just missed one.'

Rick's eyes narrowed. 'Missed what?'

'My bus,' said Elizabeth coolly.

'Bus?' Rick Masterton looked momentarily disconcerted. 'But you have your own car, surely?'

She shook her head. She preferred the freedom of public transport, walking or taking a short bus ride to the Tube station, where at least she was able to work as she travelled home. Besides, parking was a nightmare. 'No one drives in London,' she said, forcing her voice to be airy.

'Well, I do. My hire car is outside—you must let me give you a lift home——'

There was not, she realised, going to be a polite way of doing this. She turned to the commissionaire. 'Frank?' She smiled. 'Please see Mr Masterton to his car—I have a couple of papers in my office which I have to go back for.'

'Certainly, Mrs Carson.'

She turned her face to look into the darkly handsome face. 'I'll say goodnight, Mr Masterton.' And Elizabeth held out her hand towards him.

He took it, in front of the commissionaire he played his part beautifully, but Elizabeth couldn't miss the unmistakable glittering of irritation which fired at the depths of those incredible eyes.

CHAPTER TWO

ELIZABETH took the lift straight back up to her office,
her hands trembling as she sat down at her desk and
buried her head in her hands. '*Please*, God—no,' she
muttered brokenly, when the door to the adjoining room
was thrust open and there stood Jenny—an astonished
look of horror on her face.

'Mrs Carson!' she exclaimed, as she hurried over.
'Elizabeth,' she said gently. 'What is it? What's
happened?'

Elizabeth looked up unseeingly, her eyes bright.

'What is it?' repeated Jenny. 'Do you need a doctor?'

Elizabeth shut her eyes again briefly.

'You need *something*,' said Jenny firmly.

Through a cotton-wool haze, Elizabeth heard the
sounds of Jenny clattering around with bottles and
glasses and moments later a glass of pale brown liquid
was put into her hand.

'What is it?' she whispered.

'Brandy. Drink it.'

Normally calm, unflappable, in control—Elizabeth
drained the glass like an obedient child, welcoming the
warmth which licked at her stomach like fire.

Jenny sat down in the chair opposite, bolt upright, as
though she were about to take dictation. 'Do you want
to talk about it?'

Whether it was the large shot of brandy on an empty stomach, or simply the need to unburden herself to someone, she didn't know—but Elizabeth *did* want to talk.

Apart from John, she had entrusted the story to no one—for years she had been filled with a sense of shame at what had happened, but the shame had at times been punctuated with a fevered yearning for the man who had turned her from child to woman in a few short hours.

'I can't tell you,' she said quietly. 'It's too—shocking.'

Jenny gave a sad smile. 'I don't think so, my dear. I brought up a child of my own out of wedlock, remember?'

Elizabeth's eyes widened. 'You mean you knew...'

'That your husband wasn't Peter's father? Yes, I knew. Oh, just from little things you said, really. I've been working for you for a long time, remember. You *can* trust me, you know.'

'I know I can.' There was a pause. 'That man—Rick Masterton—was...is...' She looked up, her hazel eyes wide and frightened. '*He's* Peter's father, Jenny!'

She had expected some kind of appalled reaction, not Jenny's slow and thoughtful nodding of the head.

'That explains your behaviour,' she said quietly. 'But I don't understand. Today, he didn't seem to——' her voice tailed off.

'He didn't recognise me,' finished Elizabeth bitterly. 'If anything was needed to convince me that I meant nothing to him, it was our little reunion today. Because there wasn't even a flicker of recognition. That's how much I really meant to Rick Masterton.'

'Tell me about it,' said Jenny.

Elizabeth sighed as she started speaking, her voice very quiet, sounding as faraway as her thoughts. 'It all began one summer evening, almost ten years ago,' she said slowly, as the memories began to form. 'I wasn't Elizabeth then, I was Beth—and fresh out of the orphanage. I went to stay with a friend in London...'

It had been one of those magical August summer evenings, the air warm, the ice-blue sky gilded with a golden haze from the sun, when the whole world had looked a gloriously happy place, and doubly magical for Beth, who had travelled down from Wales to stay with her friend Donna who had left the orphanage the year before to live and work in London.

'I still can't believe it!' Beth had squealed fervently as she stared yet again at the slip of paper which listed her exam results.

'Well, I can!' retorted Donna. 'And you *deserve* four "A" grades and your scholarship. Imagine! I *said* you were the brightest girl that they've ever had at the orphanage, didn't I?'

'But Oxford,' said Beth, shaking her head a little as if in bemusement, so that her long pony-tail swung like a horse's tail around her long, slender neck. 'Do you suppose I'll ever fit in there?'

'With your brains, you'll fit in anywhere,' said Donna firmly. 'Now go and run a bath—we're going out to celebrate.'

'I've hardly any money——' protested Beth.

'And you won't need any—we're going to a party.'

'A party?'

'Don't look so shocked—it'll be a perfectly decent party.'

'I'm not really a party person,' said Beth doubtfully. 'Whose is it?'

'Oh, the MD's nephew is over from the States—they've hired some swanky rooms overlooking the river. They won't mind if I bring a friend.'

'Sure?'

'*Positive*!'

But 'party' seemed far too humble a description for the glittering affair which Donna took her to, thought Beth, as she hovered nervously by the picture window under which the Thames glittered slickly. She had never *seen* such a collection of exotic creatures as the guests who mingled, danced, drank champagne and laughed uproariously.

She must look terribly out of place, she thought, chewing her bottom lip a little, and if the truth were known she *felt* out of place. Donna had taken her in hand, had dressed her for the party since Beth had brought nothing suitable, and didn't have anything suitable in any case. Unfortunately, Beth was far more generously endowed that Donna, with lush, youthful curves of hip and breast. In the spangled emerald dress, her creamy breasts had spilled seductively over the bodice, making her resemble a heroine off the front cover of some historical bodice-ripper, according to Donna. 'You look quite different,' she said, her head to one side. 'And if you wore strong cool colours all the time—like this emerald, or purple, or black or blue—the colour would be reflected in your eyes. OK?'

'OK,' agreed Beth hesitantly.

'And you must wear your hair loose,' Donna insisted.

So the shiny brown hair was left to cascade in waves almost to her waist, and Beth had scarcely recognised the glittery creature who gazed back at her from the mirror. Her eyes were pale and indeterminate—usually. Muddy, Beth called them, though Donna had described them as 'hazel'. Tonight they looked completely different; Donna had been right—they were like mirrors reflecting the bright green of her dress and Donna had spiked the long, curling lashes with lots of mascara so that her face looked all eyes.

Her hand had automatically swooped down to pick up her wire-framed National Health glasses which everyone at the orphanage had teased her about, when Donna shot her a warning look and removed them from her grasp.

'No glasses. Not tonight,' she said firmly.

'But I'm as blind as a bat without them,' protested Beth.

'*Really*?' Donna looked aghast.

Beth took pity on her. 'Well, not exactly—but I can only see clearly close-up.'

'Great!' teased Donna. 'That's all you need—to be able to see the hunk you're dancing with!'

But, standing inside the elegant room at the party, staring straight ahead at the blurred crowd, she felt a bit of a fraud, wishing that she were back at the flat in her customary jeans and sweater, hair pulled back into its more usual plait, her nose deep in a book. Perhaps she could slip away unnoticed in a few minutes...

So caught up was she in her plan to escape that she scarcely noticed the man who stood a couple of feet away, also gazing out at the flamboyant sunset.

Well, that wasn't *strictly* true—of course she had *noticed* him; he had the kind of drop-dead gorgeous looks which meant that he would always have been noticed.

Most of the men there were dressed conservatively, either in suits or in casual trousers teamed with crisp, striped shirts. This man wore jeans, but with the kind of flair and panache that somehow managed to make him look the best-dressed man in the room. He wore a loose-fitting shirt which might have been silk, through which she could see a firm, hard chest, and the shirt was tucked into the jeans, displaying narrow hips and long, long legs.

She sighed as she looked away. Way, way out of *her* league. And he had a stunning-looking blonde popping titbits into his mouth.

And speaking of titbits. She still hadn't eaten.

She reached down for a triangle of toast, which was spread with something which, intriguingly, looked *black*, bit into it, began to chew, then nearly retched. It took every bit of determination she had just to swallow the morsel, but the slimy, salty taste refused to leave her mouth; then, as if in answer to a prayer, a glass of cold, clear water was placed in her hand, and she drank the whole glass thirstily before looking into an amused pair of blue-green eyes.

'I guess you're none too fond of caviar, huh?' he smiled.

He looked so darkly handsome that she had been convinced that he would be Italian, or Spanish perhaps—so that it came as something of a shock for her to hear his rich, deep American drawl.

'Caviar!' She shuddered. 'Is *that* what it is? Well, that's the first and last time *I* ever eat it!'

'Never tried it before?' He sounded curious.

She gave him a look, but then took pity on him, after all—*he* wasn't to know about the institutional food which had been the sum total of her experience. 'Actually,' she confided, the champagne she'd drunk giving her the confidence to tease, 'I normally eat it for breakfast, lunch and dinner—but this isn't Beluga, and Beluga's the only one I can bear!'

He laughed. 'But you've heard of Beluga?'

She hadn't been the light of her school debating society for nothing. 'Just because I've never tried it, it doesn't mean to say I've never heard of it!' she answered back. 'There *are* such things as books, you know!'

His eyebrows were raised slightly at the reprimand, but his eyes held a glimmer of amusement. 'I stand corrected!' He held two hands up in mock defence, then picked up a plate of *hors-d'oeuvre*. 'Here, have one of these.'

Beth eyed some more dark-looking things wrapped in bacon—yeuk!—she wasn't risking another try! She shook her head. 'No, thanks. All the books say don't eat the nibbles—they pile on the pounds and never fill you up. I'll have something when I get home.' She looked around for Donna, but he was speaking to her.

'You're not going already?'

He sounded, she thought, absolutely astonished.

She nodded. 'It's not really my scene.'

'Nor mine,' he said suddenly. 'Tell you what—I'm hungry, too. So what would you tell an American in London to eat?'

'Fish and chips out of the newspaper!' she said at once, memories of a rare seaside day-trip swamping her. 'But it's no good asking me where to find one,' she protested, as he gently but firmly pushed her through the door. 'Because I don't know London at all!'

'And neither do I,' he smiled. 'But I know a man who does.'

Which was how they found themselves in a black cab speeding towards the East End, where they were deposited in the front of the most delicious-smelling chip shop.

Still in her party clothes, but with Riccardo's jacket on, she sat with him eating their feast on a park bench, munching the hot chips covered with salt and vinegar and breaking off great chunks of glistening white cod wrapped in batter.

Then they caught a cab back to Westminster, arguing all the way about how Verdi should be interpreted. Then they went to a pub, where he tried draught bitter and found it quite as disgusting as she'd found the caviar.

Quite by coincidence they were passing underneath Big Ben when midnight struck and they stood very still as the mighty chimes rang out around them.

This is it, Cinderella, thought Beth regretfully as she stared up into that dark, beautiful face...

'Meeting him was the most magical thing that had ever happened to me,' said Elizabeth slowly, her mind coming back to the present as she surveyed Jenny sitting opposite her, staring at her with open curiosity. 'I didn't know that people like him existed—intelligent, witty—and oh, goodness, so attractive. I'd never felt any physical attraction for anyone before that—and he, somehow... he made me feel... oh, I don't know. I was stupidly naïve. Too young and too inexperienced to realise he was feeding me a line.'

'But what *happened*?' asked Jenny. 'What happened next?'

Elizabeth looked at her secretary, her eyes unwavering. 'I didn't go home that night. I went back to his uncle's flat with him. I spent the weekend there. And afterwards I discovered that I was pregnant.'

'Good grief!'

Elizabeth had expected this; the censure; perhaps that was why she had told no one besides John. 'It's pretty awful, isn't it? Not a story I'm proud of.'

Jenny shook her head. 'I'm not casting blame. For heaven's sake, you must have been so *young*.'

'Eighteen.'

'And him?'

'Twenty-five.'

'But Elizabeth—doesn't he know? About the baby?'

Elizabeth's voice became a flat monotone. 'There was no reason to tell him——'

'But surely, as the father, he had a right——'

'No!' Elizabeth's voice was harsh. 'A weekend fling with a stranger does not make you a father. It doesn't constitute any rights. And anyway——' and here her voice faltered '—I *did* try to contact him. To tell him. But he'd flown back to the States. I left him on the Sunday, and he flew back home on the Monday. And he had a fiancée back at home waiting for him. So you see,' she gave a watery smile. 'It really was just a quick roll in the hay—isn't that what Americans say?—for him.

That's all he ever intended it to be. But it gave me what has made my life worth living. It gave me Peter. Speaking of which——' and she rubbed a fist into each eye and glanced at her watch '—I'd better get going—he'll be back from football practice soon.' She swallowed the last of her brandy and got to her feet.

Jenny stood up too, still looking puzzled. 'But how could he—how could he *not* recognise you? After... after...' Her voice tailed off in embarrassment.

Elizabeth shrugged. 'It was nearly a decade ago. I'm pounds lighter, I've had my hair cropped, and I wasn't wearing glasses at the time. And, I expect,' she said bitterly, 'that there have been countless others in his bed since. But Jenny,' she said, very softly. 'Please. John was the only other person who has heard the whole story before. Perhaps I shouldn't even have told you. I probably wouldn't have done if it weren't for the shock of seeing him again. But please, promise me that you'll never speak of it to anyone? Imagine if any of the partners got to hear about it?'

'Of course I won't. Not that I think the partners would care—not in this day and age. But what about Peter? What does he know of all this? Does he think that your husband was the father?'

Elizabeth shook her head. 'No. I've never lied to him. I simply told him the truth—that I loved his Daddy very much, but that sometimes things just don't work out as you hoped they would.'

'But now that this—Rick Masterton is back. Don't you feel you ought to tell him?'

'No,' said Elizabeth with a quiet fervour. 'Not now— it's too late. *Especially* not now. I was nothing to him—

a young, willing bed-partner he can't even remember. And now he's a rich and powerful man; very powerful indeed. He's also an attorney who specialises in child custody cases, driven by a particular zealous fire—taking up the cudgels on behalf of men who he feels have been poorly treated in custody cases. Imagine if he discovers that he hasn't just been denied access, but *knowledge* of his son as well? *He could take Peter away from me.* And I can't take that chance. Now, I really must go, Jenny.' She gave a thin smile. 'Thanks for listening. I'll see you tomorrow.'

Elizabeth travelled the three blocks to the Tube station in a total daze and flashed her season ticket at the guard as she waited for the northbound train which would take her home. She took a deep breath of fresh air as she walked along the platform, welcoming the anonymity of the crowded train, the blank eyes of the fellow passengers, the opportunity the journey would give her for time to think. To come to terms with having seen him again after all this time.

But by the time she reached her exquisite detached Regent's Park house her mind was still a maze of muddled images. She walked wearily up the path to the distinctive black-painted front door, the sight of the elegant building momentarily soothing her troubled mind. Home.

She walked into the elegantly spacious hall and heard the familiar sound of a computer game from just down the hall.

'Peter!' she called, and there was a flurry as the boy, whose build, though wiry, none the less showed a hint of muscle which would make him as tall as his father in adulthood, came dashing along the corridor.

'Hello, Ma—I scored *three* times today—can you believe that? Hey——' And he peered at his mother closely. 'You haven't been *crying*, have you?'

'Crying? Of course I haven't,' said Elizabeth briskly. 'Now, do I get a hug or not?'

'*Ma*!'

He spoke with all the feigned horror of physical affection which was prevalent in little boys after their sixth birthday, but he gave her a tight hug anyway, and it needed every bit of effort she possessed for her eyes not to grow unnaturally bright for the second time that afternoon.

'Where's Mrs Clarke?' she asked, looking around for her stalwart of a housekeeper-cum-babysitter.

'Gone upstairs,' said Peter. 'She's knitting some kind of jacket for her granddaughter. What's for supper?'

Deciding on a simple supper for them both, Elizabeth went into the kitchen with Peter and busied herself with cracking eggs for omelettes and making a salad, while Peter chattered on excitedly about his chances of playing for the junior soccer team that autumn.

Elizabeth was aware that she was viewing her son with new eyes this evening. Her heart was always in her mouth when she looked at him, consumed with unconditional love for the small being whose appearance had dramatically altered the whole course of her life.

Over the years she had tried, without lasting success, not to think too much about his father, not just because of the pain, but because there didn't seem a lot of point in dwelling on a man she would never see again.

But now she had seen him, and it was as if his re-appearance had brought it slamming home to her just how like his father Peter was. The same dark hair, the same curiously light and distinctive blue-green eyes, the same long-limbed build with the potential for a distinctively steely strength. The same razor-sharp mind.

He looked up suddenly, aware of her scrutiny. 'You're sad,' he said, with unnerving perception—since she had been sure that her face showed nothing of her thoughts.

'A little,' she admitted.

'You're thinking about my dad?'

She kept her voice deliberately light. 'Why d'you say that?'

He shrugged. ''Cos that's how you always look when you think about him.' He gave a small shrug which suddenly made him look terribly vulnerable.

She felt suddenly, inexplicably guilty. 'I bet you really miss never having had a real father?' she probed.

'I had John—I can *kind* of remember him. I know he wasn't my real Dad but—he was great.'

Elizabeth remembered her ex-husband with the same affection. 'Yes, he was great. But never having known your real father——'

'You were always enough for me, Ma.' And then, obviously embarrassed by such a slushy admission, he scowled. 'When's supper going to be ready? I'm *starving*.'

'Coming right up,' she said brightly, sliding a fluffy omelette on to the plate and pushing the wooden bowl of dressed salad into the centre of the table, while they both sat down.

Nothing's going to happen, she told herself. Nothing. In a few months he'll be gone, and that will be that.

But she lay awake all night long, her face set with tension, blinking unseeingly at the moon-shadows on the ceiling, her mind fraught with images of Rick.

CHAPTER THREE

ELIZABETH'S bad night did little for her temper in the morning, and she found herself snapping at Peter more than once, something she rarely did. She was normally fairly calm where her son was concerned, and when she caught him looking at her curiously she decided to pull herself together, determined from that moment on to put away her groundless fears and to get on with life. Rick had had no part in her life for the past nine years— and there was no earthly reason why he should start now.

But what about Peter? prompted a little demon inside her head.

Peter is happy just the way he is, she told her demon tormentor fiercely.

The one good thing which had happened was that her voice had, thankfully, returned to normal.

She set off for the office to find that Jenny had already arrived; she gave Elizabeth a brisk smile and handed her a pile of correspondence, and Elizabeth breathed a small sigh of relief. Obviously Jenny was as good as her word, and last night's confidences were not about to be dredged up this morning.

Elizabeth dictated for an hour then tackled a pile of paperwork. Then she took some calls, went out for a meeting with a client, and when she came back, Jenny was sitting at her word-processor, a wry smile on her face as she pointed to a bouquet of flowers which sat on her desk. 'For you,' she said succinctly.

Elizabeth stood stock-still. She had never received flowers, never in her life, unless you counted the single red rose which Rick had had delivered on the tray containing their champagne breakfast. And she knew without looking at the card that he had sent *these* flowers, although they couldn't be more different from that simple red rose she had once so treasured.

These, she realised, were the flowers sent by a man whose tastes had matured; fragrant, subtle and lovely. There were big, squashy pale pink roses which contrasted beautifully with the clear blue of cornflowers. Peonies too, in a much darker pink. And dark green ivy nestling with the sweet-scented purple spears of lavender. A pink ribbon tied the stems together, and the whole effect was that the flowers had been freshly and casually picked in the country that morning, though this was an illusion, for Elizabeth had heard of the florist who had designed this, and knew that they charged a small fortune.

She reached down and picked up the card.

Despite the friction—or perhaps because of it—I enjoyed our encounter immensely. Have dinner with me tonight. Rick.

She crumpled the card in her hand and dropped it into the bin. She was irritated, both at the peremptory tone he'd used, and at her own brief but foolish response to his extravagant bouquet—of the sudden urge to bury her nose in the sweet perfume, to take them away to her office and arrange them lovingly in a vase. I should trample them underfoot, she thought bitterly, as common sense prevailed.

'You can have the flowers, Jenny,' she said abruptly. 'Or send them downstairs to the typing pool.'

'Are you sure?' Jenny's eyes were assessing. 'They're from Mr Masterton, aren't they?'

'Yes, they are, and yes, I'm sure—and if he rings—you can tell him——'

But her words were never to be spoken, for at that moment Paul Meredith, her boss, had strolled smilingly through the door.

'Tell him what? Mmm—lovely flowers. Yours, Elizabeth?'

Elizabeth nodded.

There was a gleam in Paul's eyes. 'And may we know who they're from?'

Elizabeth was reluctant to tell him, but she wasn't about to start lying to her boss. 'They're from Rick Masterton,' she said stiffly.

'You obviously made quite a hit,' he observed.

'You sound surprised,' said Elizabeth, a trifle waspishly.

Paul's eyebrows rose. 'The only thing that surprises me is why someone didn't sweep you off your feet years ago. I've tried often enough!'

Elizabeth smiled. Over the years, Paul had frequently asked her out, but she had said no so often to him that she suspected he wouldn't be able to cope if she gave him a positive answer! A divorcé, in his early forties, with an easygoing manner which carefully hid his astute business mind, Paul was an eligible man, but Elizabeth had no intention of dating her boss—that was simply asking for trouble, quite apart from the fact that she simply didn't fancy him. I don't fancy *anyone*, she thought gloomily. Except Rick.

'So where are you having dinner?'

'I'm not.' She saw his perplexed frown. 'Having dinner, that is.' She turned to her secretary. 'Please tell Mr Masterton that quite clearly, when he calls.'

Paul walked through into her office and Elizabeth followed.

He turned to face her. 'Why not?' he asked.

It was pointless acting dense with such an astute man as Paul, and yet she was stuck for a legitimate excuse that wouldn't have her reputation in tatters around her feet. She could imagine Paul's reaction if she told him the truth. Actually, Paul, he's the father of my child and he doesn't know and I don't want him to find out and upset my world for the second time.

Paul noted her silence with a further frown. 'You have a date?'

'No.' He knew the absence of dates in her life.

'Peter, then? Trouble with babysitters? Is your house-keeper going out?'

'No, Paul,' she said heavily. 'Nothing like that.'

'What, then? He's a valuable client, and you've dined with clients before. Why not go?'

'Is that an order?' She met his gaze steadily.

He looked back at her with equal calm. 'I don't know, Elizabeth—does it need to be?'

She knew he was joshing her, so she forced a smile as she ran her fingers back through her short, shiny hair. 'If you must know—I'm still feeling a bit scratchy after my bout of the flu——'

Paul smacked a hand to his brow. 'Hell, I'm sorry—why didn't you say?' He gave her a rueful smile. 'I just thought that it's the kind of opportunity that most women wouldn't turn down, even if they were dead on their feet. When I was in the States last year Rick had to virtually fight them off in droves. I guess that's why we all think you're so amazing—you're so unpredictable.'

She laughed. 'I'm not sure that sounds like a compliment! Now, Paul——' she gave him her most efficient smile '—did you want to see me about anything in particular?'

'I wanted to talk to you about the Haynes case. Do you have the file?'

'Sure do.' It was with relief that Elizabeth was able to lose herself in the intricacies of the complicated accounts of the Haynes Company—made doubly complex by the sudden departure of the company secretary, who had, it transpired, been cooking the books.

Ater Paul had left her office Elizabeth worked flat-out until almost three, and was just thinking about finding herself a cup of coffee when the phone on her desk rang. 'Hello,' she said.

There was a silence on the other end of the phone. 'Hello,' she said again. And then, when the silence continued, 'Is anyone there?'

There was another pause. Then, 'Is that you, Mrs Carson?'

'Yes, Mr Masterton,' she said instantly, and could have bitten her tongue off. She would have recognised that deep voice any time and anywhere but why let *him* know that?

'You have a good memory for names and voices, considering we only just met,' he observed with chilling accuracy, his voice sounding very slightly harsh. 'I'll bet you don't greet everyone by name without having it announced to you.'

She twisted her pen round in her fingers. 'Not all my clients have American accents.'

'I'll bet they don't.'

Something in his tone made her uneasy. Her heart was beating with frightening speed. 'Was there something in particular you wanted to ask me, Mr Masterton?'

Again, that cold, flat tone. 'Let's say you just answered it,' he said ominously, and then there was a click as he hung up.

'Mr Masterton! Mr Masterton!' repeated Elizabeth foolishly, sounding like a harried telephonist. She replaced the receiver with a trembling hand.

Now why had he hung up?

She shook her head, trying to put him out of her mind. Ignore him, she thought. *Ignore* him. And she picked up her pen and began to write.

But it was no good. The feeling of foreboding persisted. Oh, why had Jenny just put him straight through? she wondered desperately. Because you insist that all clients be put through. It's part of your 'hands on' policy—and you'd have been angry if she'd done otherwise. Or would she?

A stupidly irrational fear that he might come to the office just would not go away. She even buzzed through to Jenny, who came in immediately.

'If Mr Masterton appears, then let me know immediately, would you, Jenny?'

'But you aren't expecting him, are you?'

'I—no. No, I'm not.' I'm just being paranoid.
Imagining things, Elizabeth told herself.

At five-thirty she told Jenny to go and began to pack
up. She looked out of the window. It was a fine, clear
May evening. The walk to the Tube would do her good—
with a bit of luck it would blow all the cobwebs away,
and with them the persistent misgivings which wouldn't
leave her.

There was a sound behind her. A soft sound—of
footfall on carpet, of expelled breath. She felt the tiny
hairs prickle on the back of her neck.

'Hello, Beth,' he said, very, very softly.

She didn't move for a moment, sucked in her own
breath, felt the blood leave her face, an icy blanch replacing it. But it was not shock she felt, no indeed—for
she had subconsciously been expecting just this since the
moment he'd hung up. Not shock.

Fear.

She turned around, her mind buzzing like a crazed
moth around a lightbulb as she searched frantically for
the right thing to say.

His eyes were cold, his face carved from granite.

She regressed. Fear made her a child again, her years
of self-possession vanquished by those two words of his.
The adult fought the child in her and the child won.
Because only a child would have attempted to play ignorant against such a devastating opponent.

'I beg your pardon?' She'd got it just right—the
undertone of amusement, the slight rise of her
elegant eyebrows.

The mouth twisted into a cold smile. 'You don't re-member?' he mocked. 'Then maybe I ought to remind you?'

Dazed and confused, a sick kind of excitement now vying with fear for domination, she hardly registered that he was approaching her with stealthy intent.

She might have been a waxwork, she stood so still, unable to move as he reached her, stood looking down at her, his eyes glittering as coldly as some rare jewel, his firm mouth curved into a cruel imitation of a smile.

'Shall I remind you?' he queried. '*Beth*.'

And then the dark head swooped, and he claimed her mouth with a sensual arrogance which was irresistible.

Her lips parted immediately, automatically. Oh, the sweet, heady pressure of his mouth, setting up a shock-ingly instant response deep within her. His tongue began to explore the outline of her lips, as though he were re-membering her by taste alone, and her hands went up to grip the broad shoulders, afraid that if she didn't cling on to something she would fall to her knees before him. She heard him make some small sound of assertion at the back of his throat and then he deepened the kiss and she gave a little, anguished cry—wishing that it could have stayed like this, that the long, lonely years in be-tween had never happened.

He stopped kissing her then, as abruptly as he had started. They stood facing one another, the only sound their frantically laboured breathing as they both fought to drag air back into their empty lungs. But he recovered before she did, and stepped back a little, surveying her still with that cool air of assessment.

'Still the same old Beth,' he said insultingly. 'Such a response. Just press the right buttons, and up she goes in flames! Did that get the old memory banks jumping?' he mocked. 'Or perhaps you'd like me to remind you some more.' His eyes travelled slowly from neck to ankle, lingering on the full curve of her breasts the longest. 'This reawakening could be so good—don't you think?'

She had wanted him to kiss her, and her need had allowed her to conveniently ignore his cold, unsmiling face. But she could not ignore his deliberately insulting words. If any other man had behaved in the way that he had just done, she would have hit his face. But not this man.

Fleetingly she wondered just why he was so angry with her. Just a girl from way back. But the answer came to her instantly—no doubt she had wounded his pride by slipping away that morning. He was obviously one of those men who liked to do the leaving. Probably would have liked her to accompany him to the airport, flushed and rosy after forty-eight hours of non-stop love-making. To have stood in the departure lounge waving her little hanky as he roared off out of her life. Her mouth compressed itself into a straight line as she remembered his duplicity.

'Get out,' she said, and he laughed.

'Out?' he queried softly. 'Oh, no, Beth. You and I have some talking to do.'

She fought to regain some sort of authority. 'My name is Elizabeth,' she snapped. Beth was gone forever. Beth was too soft, too trusting, too vulnerable. Elizabeth was cool and capable. Wasn't she?

He shook his head. 'Not to me. I might call you Elizabeth, but to me you'll always be Beth. Passionate Beth; as sweet and ripe as a peach.' His voice lowered, deliberately provocative. 'And just perfect for picking.'

She shivered in spite of herself. 'Riccardo. Please——'

'Ah! So you *do* remember.'

'Of course I remember.'

'That's good. For a moment there I thought that I'd been overestimating myself for all these years.'

Colour rose to her cheeks at the sexual boast. Sickened, she felt consumed by a fleeting primeval rush of jealousy, as she thought of all the women he must have had before her. And since. She had to get out of here. She'd humiliated herself enough in front of him for one day. 'I have to go,' she said dully, but he shook his head.

'Oh, no,' he said grimly. 'You and I are going to talk.'

She thought of Peter at home, waiting for her. His son! She shook her head. 'I—I can't.'

'Why not?'

And of course, she couldn't tell him the reason why. She hesitated.

'You have another date?'

She seized on this eagerly. 'That's right.'

'Then cancel it.' He spoke with all the arrogant conviction of a man who knew that a woman *would* cancel a date at the drop of a hat just to be with him.

'It isn't just that.'

'You have a child at home, perhaps?'

Her heart stilled. She thought of Peter and she play-acted bemusement brilliantly. Some instinct told her not to lie. 'Yes, I do. How did you know that?'

He shrugged. 'Paul mentioned it. In passing.'

Damn Paul! Damn him! But thank God, in a sense that he'd found out that way. Imagine—imagine if he'd seen Peter himself. Another polished smile. 'So now you understand why I can't have that drink with you?'

He shrugged with careless ease. 'No problem. We'll go to your place. I'd be interested to meet any child of *yours*, Beth.'

'You can't,' she told him, a little too quickly, then, seeing his face, rushed on. 'I mean—I try not to take boyfriends home while he's awake.' She saw his mouth twist in comprehension, and although it sickened her to do so, she compounded the lie still further. 'He's a light sleeper,' she confided. 'And——' her voice held a con-spiratorial tone '—the slightest noise wakens him.'

The implication behind her words was rawly shocking, and the look of utter disgust on his face was so marked that she actually thought he was about to leave, but then she saw his glance flick to the swell of her breasts, the glimpse of lace just faintly discernible through the thin white silk blouse.

'Poor kid,' he muttered, half under his breath. 'Can't you get a sitter?' he said, more harshly. 'Who's looking after him now?'

It didn't occur to her to stem his interrogation; she was too frightened of the weapon he unwittingly wielded—paternal rights. Too frightened of what he might do if he found out. And terrified of his reputation for winning custody cases.

'Who's looking after him?' he repeated, as she continued to stare at him mutely.

'I have a live-in housekeeper. She looks after Peter when I'm working.'

'Then call her. Tell her you're going to be late. Come on, Beth,' he drawled, with a long, lazy smile and she saw the sexual hunger in his eyes, despised it, even while it stirred something deep within herself. 'You know you want to.'

She sensed then his determination—recognised that he wouldn't let up, that his curiosity had been aroused, that—and his libido. Wouldn't it be simpler just to go? He obviously disapproved of the person he thought she'd become, maybe she could make him disapprove of her a little more, so that an evening out was hardly likely to become a regular thing. Why not get it over with?

She stared at him coolly. 'Just a drink, then.'

He gave a grim kind of smile, as though the victory meant little to him. 'Let's go.'

'I have to telephone. Would you mind waiting outside?'

He hesitated, then shrugged. 'OK.'

It took only a couple of minutes to ring Mrs Clarke, who was, as always, absolutely delighted to keep her eye on Peter, telling Elizabeth cheerfully to be as late as she liked.

But I don't want to be as late as I like, thought Elizabeth, with a sinking heart as she pulled a comb through the neat shiny crop of her hair, and went through to the outer office to find Rick sitting on Jenny's desk, his stance languidly at ease, his eyes curious as he watched her walk in.

He stood up. 'Let's go.'

She was silent as they went down in the lift, wondering if she was doing the most stupid thing of her life. Or the second most stupid.

Although not a native of the city, he seemed to know exactly where he was going, taking her to a bar just a few minutes' walk away, a place entirely new to her.

She felt him watching her intently as she sank down on to the cream banquette. A waitress came over to him immediately; he was that kind of man. The waitress looked like an off-duty actress, thought Elizabeth as she ordered a glass of wine. She found herself comparing the woman's cascading blonde hair with her own short, shiny crop, catching sight of herself in the smoked mirror, at the neat linen suit with the slim-fitting skirt, the short hair, the big glasses. Whereas I, she thought wryly, look exactly what I am—a dull office worker.

And then her eyes met his in the mirror for a long moment.

'You've changed, Elizabeth,' he said, pronouncing the unabbreviated version of her name for the first time with sardonic emphasis, and stupidly—this hurt.

'Have I?'

He studied her with dispassionate appraisal. 'You sure have. You've cut off all that thick hair; slimmed down, too.'

'I was never fat,' she said, with a touch of defiance.

'No. But you were curvy. Now you're very streamlined. Very cool, and very sophisticated. And, of course, I've never seen you with glasses.'

'Is that why you didn't recognise me?'

He leaned back against the banquette, smiled his thanks at the waitress who lovingly deposited a dish of mixed nuts in front of him and shook his head. 'No. It was your voice that did it,' he said, and again Elizabeth caught an angry spark in his eyes.

'My voice?'

'Sure. People can change out of all recognition, but their voices remain constant. But your voice had changed. You've lost your Welsh accent, for one thing. And your voice was much deeper, very husky. *Ve-ry* sexy.'

She disregarded that. 'I'd just recovered from a bout of flu.'

'I see.' The light returned to his eyes as they flicked over her briefly. 'You've changed,' he said again.

She looked at him directly. 'I know. I'm no longer so—*rash*.' Years of hurt pride, of a struggle to forget him which had threatened to drag her down on more than one occasion, made her linger on the word, so that he would know exactly what she meant.

His eyes were cold, the voice strangely gritty. 'I see. And is that all our weekend meant to you—a moment of rashness?'

She remembered how it had ended. How dared he be critical of her, when all the time he'd been making love to her, he'd had a fiancée at home waiting for him? And he would never know of the tears she had wept over him. Never. Her pride simply wouldn't allow him to. 'Of course,' she said lightly. 'Surely you didn't imagine anything else?'

She saw something starkly angry in his eyes as the waitress brought her wine, his beer. She sipped at it gratefully, holding on to the glass with fingers which felt like slabs of ice.

The silence which grew didn't seem to concern him in the slightest; he simply watched her as he sipped his drink. It was impossible to read anything in that darkly handsome face—and even if she had thought she could, she would not have trusted her perception. Because once before she had read what she had believed to be love in those glittering eyes, and in that she had been way, way off the mark.

'So. Tell me about yourself, Elizabeth. Fill in the years.'

She pretended she was at an interview. Present the facts concisely. 'Much of it you know. I'm an accountant, widowed—with one son.'

He sipped his drink. 'How old is your son?'

'He's seven,' she lied brightly.

He nodded. 'And your husband died—recently?'

'John died four years ago.'

'I'm sorry.'

She met his eyes. Are you? 'He was a good man,' she said quietly, and saw his mouth twist before he swallowed a mouthful of beer.

'And you married—when?'

She named the month; the year.

His face hardened. 'Busy year for you, then. So many men.'

She ignored the slur, but with it had come the kind of insolently candid appraisal he had subjected her to in her office. He was staring with open interest at the discreet gleam of pale gold which shone at her wrist and ears.

'A rich husband, judging by the baubles you wear. You married well, Elizabeth?'

Yes, she had married well, but the marriage had certainly not been made in heaven. If only he knew. 'I'm no gold-digger!' she snapped. 'And I don't intend to sit here and be insulted by your not very subtle inferences.'

He shrugged. 'The facts speak for themselves, surely? You hot-footed it from my bed to this other guy's, and within months you were out tossing the rice.'

She turned on him, unable to fault him without giving herself away. 'It's a free country,' she said coldly, and she saw a muscle of distaste move in his cheek. She wanted to stand up and shout out that she *knew* about his fiancée, that she'd actually spoken to her on the phone, but pride forbade her to disclose it. Why should she let him know how she'd suffered? Let him believe that *she* had been the one to break it off.

She saw him frown and she suddenly knew that she couldn't talk to him any more, that she had no wish to pursue the answers to questions it was better remained unasked. Fleetingly she wondered whether he had married the fiancée. He wore no wedding band, but then, so few men did these days.

She put her drink down heavily on the smoked glass table, and as she stood up, he followed suit, completely dwarfing her with his height.

'I have to go.'

'You haven't finished your drink.'

'I don't want it.'

'Here.' He bent down to pick up her slim leather clutch bag which lay forgotten on the banquette, tucking it underneath her elbow, and just that brief contact scorched through her. He felt it too, she could see that from the way his eyes darkened, the brief flare of the autocratic nostrils and her eyelids fell to cover her confusion that he should still respond to her so instantly.

They stood in the doorway and Elizabeth stared in dismay at the light shower which was covering all the cars and hurrying homegoers with fine drizzle. Brollies had already risen—dark hulks blotting out the sky. And she had left the office without hers.

'My car's near by. Let me bring it round. I'll drive you home.'

She had to stop this right now. He was playing with her, manipulating her, as once he'd done so long ago. '*No*!' She hadn't even realised that she'd shouted until she saw a couple whirl round and stare at her. 'It's no good, Rick. Don't you understand? Let's let the past lie buried,' she hurled at him, and set off through the rain.

But in her high heels she was no match for him; he was hot on her trail and she heard him behind her before he caught hold of her shoulders, pulling her roughly into his arms, so that her bag flew from beneath her elbow and on to the pavement at their feet, spilling its contents all over the place, though neither of them moved to retrieve it.

The drizzle had spangled his dark hair, dripping down the tanned cheeks, the tiny drops joining to form rivulets, and she felt a rivulet on her own cheek, like a tear.

His eyes seared into her.

'Let me go,' she gasped weakly. 'Everything's changed.'

He said nothing, just pulled her to him and kissed her again.

The effect of it was as numbing as an intravenous drug—impossible to fight; impossible to resist. The rain on their faces mingled in union as did their lips, their tongues, their bodies.

She felt her body glue itself to his. It fitted so well there, as though they had been designed to each complement the other. Not that she had anything to compare it with—there had only ever been him, like this. And the thought of her laughable innocence made her try to pull away, but she couldn't. And it wasn't anything to do with the fact that he had his hand placed firmly at the small of her back, making their hips meld with shocking intimacy. She couldn't move because she didn't want to. She wanted to forget reality and lose herself in this frightening pleasure.

Briefly he lifted his mouth away from hers to look down at her, the light eyes glittering, the warmth of his breath against her lips. 'Nothing's changed.' It was an arrogant assumption. And true. 'Tell me you don't want me, Elizabeth,' he whispered mockingly. 'You can't, can you?' But the taunt did not make her shrink away from him in shame, because she sensed that, just for those few moments while they rediscovered how good their kisses had always been, he, too, had been as much a victim of his own desire as she was.

He bent his head and kissed her again, and Elizabeth moaned, but it was a moan of desire, not of protest. Oblivious to the stares of the passers-by, they clung to each other feverishly, and Elizabeth was so caught up in the throes of it all that it took several seconds for her to realise that he was releasing her, looking down at her with eyes that flashed fire, a lazy smile curving his mouth.

'Some things never change, do they?' he said, then bent his head to her ear to whisper, 'Let's go somewhere quiet, somewhere we won't be disturbed—come back to my hotel with me.' His voice became a harsh note. 'We need to talk, Elizabeth.'

Her dream world disintegrated. She felt faint at his suggestion that she go back with him to his hotel. Talk? That was a new name for what *he* evidently had in mind, she thought bitterly. The bubble burst and she was back where she started, only worse. After all that had happened the attraction remained, and she wondered what sort of dolt she must be, still to be physically affected by him after all these years?

And yet he too, she thought grimly, as she stared back at him, he evidently felt exactly the same way about her, too.

For wasn't he offering her the same as he had done then? No more? No less? But at least this time he hadn't been so hypocritical as to dress up his lust with words she had mistakenly thought meant that he loved her...

'Elizabeth,' he said softly, and made to pull her into his arms again, but she pushed him away with a strength she didn't know she possessed.

'Sorry, Rick, but the answer's no. I don't shack up with strange men any more,' she said coldly.

His mouth twisted, a strange light glowing in the depths of his blue-green eyes. 'You think that's what I want?' he queried in a soft voice which dripped danger.

'What else am I supposed to think?' she asked bitterly. 'That's all it was last time, wasn't it?'

She was startled by the alien look which momentarily transformed his features into some bleak and drawn countenance she barely recognised.

'Is that what you think?' he gritted. 'Is that why you ran out on me?'

For one second she was tempted to tell him the truth, to describe the cruel way in which she'd discovered his duplicity. But if she told him, wouldn't it reopen the wound she had hoped had healed? Why should her pride be bruised still further?

She drew her shoulders back as she stared at him. 'Let's just say, I realised that I'd made a mistake, and I couldn't think of a way to tell you.' She saw a muscle angrily contract in his cheek. 'As I said, let's leave the past where it belongs.' And then, afraid that he would see the tears welling up in her eyes, she scrabbled around at his feet in the rain, retrieving her handbag and its scattered contents, then turned and fled, a crowd of people fortuitously filing out from an early showing at the cinema thankfully swallowing her up, so that she could slip away unnoticed.

CHAPTER FOUR

THE next two days were hell.

Elizabeth tried to carry on as normal, hoping that no one else had noticed the tense expectation which had stretched her nerves to pieces, while at home she made a determined effort to shield Peter from her fears.

Two days had passed since that appallingly public display, when Rick had kissed her so thoroughly in full view of all the curious passers-by, just minutes from her office. Two days, and not a second had gone by when he hadn't been on her mind.

She felt deflated and confused, knowing that her overriding emotion *should* be one of relief—that he had taken her at her word and decided to leave her alone. So why wasn't it? Because she was still, albeit unwillingly, overwhelmingly attracted to the man?

And these feelings were coupled with a nagging guilt which just wouldn't go away. For wasn't it profoundly wrong to deny a man the knowledge of the existence of his son? Perhaps his only son?

But a chill iced her skin whenever the guilt emerged, for she remained nervous of Rick—and of his power, as a man, and as an attorney. She thought of the two famous palimony cases he had won recently, against all the odds. As though trying to torment herself, she had had transcripts of the trials faxed through to her, which had only confirmed her suspicions. That, in court, Rick was as deadly and as ruthless as a cobra.

And what if she *did* tell him about Peter? Even given the least damaging scenario of him blithely accepting her silence on the matter for all these years, he would hardly just nod, see Peter once, and then just disappear.

No. She knew enough of Rick to know that he would want to be *involved* in his son's life, and therefore in hers—and that would be much, much too painful.

Selfish, mocked a voice. Selfish coward.

I'm not! she defended herself silently. But none the less she couldn't stop herself imagining the worst possible scenario—that he would use all his wealth and his power and his skill to take Peter away from her....

However, by Saturday morning she had allowed her frail hopes to grow into certainty that he intended to leave her alone.

She rose early—sleep had been at a premium of late—and dressed in faded jeans and an old plaid shirt in shades of emerald and sage, which picked out the green lights in her hazel eyes. She had washed her hair, leaving the short style to dry naturally, so that it appeared much softer than the blow-dried version she sported at the office. Having to always appear sleek and smart at work, at weekends she tended to rebel a bit, dressing in a scruffy manner which delighted her son because it meant that chocolatey or muddy fingers inadvertantly smeared all over her clothes wouldn't make her turn a hair!

Just before nine she walked Peter to the park, where a weekly supervised football session was about to commence. She stood on the sidelines with the other mothers and fathers, faithfully applauding her son's team, and shouting fit to burst when Peter headed a goal home. On the way home, as had become their little tradition, they stopped off to buy her newspaper, his comic, and some chocolate croissants.

They had settled down to enjoy them in the sunny kitchen with its pale oak units and its french windows leading out on to the flower-filled patio, when there was a sharp ring at the doorbell.

She rose to leave her cooling coffee to answer it, hoping that it wasn't yet another of the salesmen who seemed to haunt this area.

It wasn't.

She opened the door to find Rick there, and his eyes narrowed as he saw her, and she found herself wishing that she weren't dressed in her oldest clothes, her face all bare and rosy—it made her feel strangely naked and vulnerable, and that was the *last* thing she wanted to feel. 'What—what are you doing here?' she whispered.

The only answer he gave to her question was to allow his eyes to rove over the elegant white porticos of the exquisitely designed house. 'Nice place you have here,' he drawled insultingly. 'I guess you earned it pretty well.'

Her lips tightened proudly as she understood his implication. 'What are you doing here?' she asked quietly.

He leaned insolently against one of the porticos. 'So, Elizabeth,' he drawled. 'I believe you married a very rich man indeed. John Carson.'

'How did you know that?' she queried, more urgency in her voice than she had intended.

He looked at her as though she were a complete idiot. 'There are always ways and means; surely you know that?'

'You've had me *investigated*?'

He gave a cold smile. 'Don't be so melodramatic, Elizabeth. I asked around, that's all, picked up a few facts. And very interesting facts they were, too. Understandable, I suppose, that your tastes should run to a man who was worth about a hundred times what I was at the time. Though, by the look of him—it doesn't appear that he was offering me much in the way of competition in the—er—shall we say—physical stakes. Just a little on the ancient side for you, wasn't he, honey?'

'Don't you dare speak ill of the dead,' she answered furiously.

'I'd have said it while he was alive,' he retorted. 'Because it's true. An old man, and a beautiful young girl. And there's only one bartering tool in that equation, isn't there? Money. And lots of it.'

'John wasn't that old!' she protested, stung. 'He was only thirty-eight.'

'And you were—what—eighteen?' he mocked.

Don't rise to it, she thought. Get rid of him. 'That too is none of your business,' she said sweetly. Then, very coolly, because a sudden fear had begun to torment her, 'Why are you here?'

'So touchy, Elizabeth,' he observed. 'Does the sight of me disturb you so much?' The blue-green eyes looked almost luminous in the olive complexion. He was dressed casually this morning, in caramel-coloured cords and a beautifully cut cream linen shirt. The morning sunshine spilled on to the dark head so that it gleamed blue-black. 'Aren't you going to invite me inside?'

Her upper arms, though encased in the thick plaid of her shirt, became alive with goose-bumps. She thought of Peter, sitting eating his croissants. 'You—can't,' she stumbled.

'Oh?' The direction of his eyes travelled lazily over her shoulder to the interior of the house.

What she ought to do was to slam the door in his face, but she didn't dare try.

'I told you. My son is here. It isn't fair to him.'

The mouth twisted. 'But surely, even *you*, Elizabeth—have men *friends*. Your objection was, as I recall—that you didn't want to risk waking him.' He glanced at his own watch. 'As I now make it just after eleven in the morning, there is little chance of that happening.' He smiled. A very cold smile indeed. 'Is there?'

'Who is it, Mum?'

Elizabeth stilled, frozen into immobility.

'Mum?'

She heard the scrape of a chair, the sound of footsteps. Yet still she could not move, she was caught up in a cold vice of inevitability, and she realised that she had been waiting for this moment to happen since the moment that Rick had walked back into her life. And, crazily, for her child's sake—hadn't there always been a tiny part of her that had always wanted this?

Peter must have sensed something in the atmosphere, for he did not approach at anything like his normal fireball speed. Long and gangly, he came at them cautiously—like a child introduced to Father Christmas for the first time.

Elizabeth was just the observer, the outsider in the scene which was being played out before her eyes.

She heard the sudden inrush of breath, the only outward sign of emotion on Rick's part because he too was still, just as still as she was.

There was open curiosity on Peter's face as he registered a tall man with exactly the same unusual eye-colour which stared back at him from the mirror when he bothered to look in it.

For one moment of utter madness, Elizabeth almost thought that they were going to hurl themselves into each other's arms in an open display of familial recognition, but of course they didn't.

She heard Rick's sharp intake of breath, heard the soft words muttered quickly and low in the Italian he'd only ever spoken while making love to her. He raised his eyes to her face. They asked her a question to which she knew she could never give lie to. Almost imperceptibly, she nodded, and he expelled the breath he had been holding in a long, slow hiss, before turning to look at Peter.

Peter spoke first. 'Hello,' he said shyly. 'I'm Peter.'

'Hi, Peter,' said Rick very softly, his eyes never leaving the boy's face. 'I'm Rick.'

'You're *American*!' crowed Peter in delight, then turned to face his mother. 'You didn't tell me you had any *American* friends!' he accused.

Elizabeth still couldn't speak. She looked at Rick. Don't tell him, beseeched her eyes, and then she almost recoiled from the look of cold, hard fury she saw in his own eyes.

He crouched down to Peter's level. 'That's because she didn't know she still had any,' he smiled. 'I haven't seen your Mom in a long time.'

'Oh.' He looked at him again. 'Can you ride a horse?' asked Peter suspiciously.

'Sure can.'

'And shoot a gun?'

Rick laughed—a deep, spontaneous chuckle which had once sent shivers of delight down Elizabeth's spine.

'I can,' he said gently. 'I choose not to. Guns are for cowboy movies.'

'I *like* cowboy movies,' Peter ventured, then smiled, and Elizabeth's heart almost broke in two to witness her normally diffident son warm to the stranger who was really his father, like a flower opening to the morning sun.

'Darling, have you finished your breakfast?' asked Elizabeth gently, pathetically clinging to the vain hope that Rick might still leave them in peace. They both looked up at her in unison. Intruder. Again that cold look of silent rage was directed at her.

'I'm not hungry,' said Peter immediately.

'Your Mom and I were just arranging to take you out on a picnic.'

'A *picnic*! Oh, Mum—when? When?'

Steely eyes unnerved her. 'We were thinking of this afternoon, weren't we, Beth?'

'*Beth*?' exclaimed Peter. 'Nobody calls her Beth. She's Elizabeth.'

But this time he went unanswered, for Rick's eyes were on Elizabeth's face.

'Weren't we, Elizabeth?' he repeated silkily, the warning there for only her to hear.

She nodded, her heart in her mouth, cold terror filling her veins as she acknowledged the extent of her deception, and what he must be thinking of her. 'Yes, Rick,' she faltered. He held, she thought with a sinking feeling—all the cards.

'And is your housekeeper free this evening?' he continued.

'This evening?' she echoed foolishly.

'Why, yes, Elizabeth,' he spoke deliberately. 'We need a sitter for tonight because I'm taking you out. You and I have a lot to talk about.'

'I—Peter——' She stared helplessly at her son, but Rick had pre-empted her, looking down at the boy with a gentle smile on his lips.

'You don't mind if I take your Mom out for dinner this evening, do you, Peter? We have a lot of catching up to do.' His tone was very adult, it conveyed a sense of man-to-man, and Peter picked up on this immediately.

Peter shook his head. 'Of course I don't mind. You go, Mum—and have a good time.'

Elizabeth could have laughed at this strangely new grown-up stance. Or cried. But if she cried she might never stop.

'Now, Peter,' said Rick softly. 'Do you think you can get the picnic ready? Can you make sandwiches?'

'Of course I can!' boasted Peter. 'I *am* nearly nine, you know!'

'Yes,' said Rick flatly. 'I know.'

Peter ran off towards the kitchen and further colour drained from Elizabeth's cheeks as she recalled how blithely she'd lied about her son's age. Alone now, in the hallway with Rick, she stared up at him white-faced.

He gripped her forearm with a ferocity which made her wince. 'Where's the living-room?' he interrogated harshly.

She pointed. 'Over there,' she said weakly.

Unceremoniously he hauled her into the room she had indicated and almost threw her down on to the sofa. He walked over to the window and stood gazing out of it for several minutes before turning to face her, and she recoiled from the dark anger which had hardened the already harsh angles of his face.

'You told me your son was seven,' he bit out savagely. 'You lied to me!'

'Yes.' What was the point of denying it? She felt strangely calm, as though someone had emptied her of all feelings, leaving nothing but a shell behind.

There was silence for a moment. 'So, *Elizabeth*—just how many others are privy to this little secret of yours? This really is a case of the father being the last to know, isn't it?'

'Apart from my husband—my secretary is the only person I've told,' she replied calmly. 'And then only recently.'

He came a little closer and lowered his voice. 'I *am* the father, I take it, Elizabeth? My eyes did not deceive me back there?'

She tried to think about the best way to handle this, but all her reasoning powers seemed to have deserted her. 'Yes, you are,' she admitted quietly.

'And if—Peter's resemblance to me had not been so remarkable, if for example he had been all of you, and nothing of me—then would you have told me? Or was I to remain in ignorance of his existence forever?'

This she didn't want to answer. It was already painful enough for her to admit to herself that she had tried to keep Peter hidden from his father. And yet she wanted him to get some inkling of the self-protective instincts which had governed her behaviour. 'Rick, I want to say——'

'Say *nothing*,' he interrupted harshly, looking quickly over his shoulder, as though Peter might walk in at any moment and hear them arguing. 'Nothing which could upset the boy. You will have every opportunity to speak. Tonight. Now——' he must have heard Peter approaching, because he injected a warm note into his voice '—hadn't you better bring some sweaters, Elizabeth? For you and Peter? I know how unreliable your British weather can be?'

And their eyes met, the conventional comment turned into something else entirely as a flash of recognition sparked between them, and she remembered a party on a sunny summer's evening—the first after weeks of rain, a whole lifetime ago...

'Cinderella,' Riccardo whispered, uncannily echoing Beth's thoughts as the deep, resonant chimes of Big Ben died away on the twelfth stroke.

And, being Prince Charming, he would have to kiss her, she thought dreamily, closing her eyes quite instinctively, and he enveloped her in his arms, capturing her lips in a long first kiss which Beth would have defied anyone in the world to have bettered. She clung to him and kissed him back, fervently conveying every emotion she had suppressed over years in the cold atmosphere of the orphanage, but the most overriding emotion of all was something so powerful that it set her on fire for him. She wanted, she realised, quite without shock—she wanted him to love her...*as she loved him*.

She shook her head a little. Now she was going crazy—she'd only just *met* the guy, for heaven's sake!

But she didn't pull away when he gave a small groan, and pressed his hard body against hers and whispered into her ear. 'God, I don't want you to go home.'

She looked up at him with untroubled eyes, a secret dreamy smile flicking over her parted lips. 'I don't have to,' she whispered back. Then realised that it was *her* talking, simple, inexperienced Beth, and her voice trembled uncertainly. 'If you're sure——'

'*Sure*?' For a moment he looked incredulous, and then his face darkened. 'I want you so badly, Beth, but...'

'But?' she prompted, heart in her mouth, afraid that he was going to reject her.

He stared down at her for a long moment. 'It's difficult to explain,' he admitted. 'The timing's all wrong——'

She knew that he was being a gentleman, adored him even more for it, and gave a little smile, as if deferring judgement. You're the expert, her eyes said trustingly as she gave a little nod of her head. But the movement caused her breasts to rise, their swollen creaminess threatening to spill out of the confines of the too-small bodice, and he made a small sound in the back of his throat before taking her hand in his, holding it up to his lips and kissing it.

'Let's get out of here,' he said urgently.

Through the hours that followed, Beth did not have a single regret as he took her to bed and made love to

her with passion and reverence and care...except for
that one time in the middle of that first night when,
drowsy and warm, they had become locked in an em-
brace which was impossible to break, and impossible to
stop—when his lovemaking had been tinged with something approaching desperation.

He hadn't guessed she had been a virgin, and she
hadn't told him, because she had sensed that something
troubled him, and that in some way he had offended
some moral code of honour in taking her to his bed. At
least she assumed that was why a faraway, almost
brooding expression made his unbearably handsome face
look almost savage as he lowered his body on to hers
and took her to paradise and back in the slowest and
most delicious way imaginable.

They spent the whole weekend in the flat. 'It's my
uncle's,' he explained, when she questioned him. 'He
and my aunt use it when they're staying in London.
Thank God——' and his eyes twinkled '—that he was
due to fly to Paris the night of the party. The gods must
be on our side, Elizabeth.'

Oh, they must be, she prayed.

It was certainly a most luxurious flat, the most costly
setting she could have imagined, and yet Elizabeth
scarcely seemed to notice the exquisite paintings, the vast
marble floors with their silk rugs—she was far too en-
raptured with this man. Her man.

They picnicked on the floor. Made love on the floor;
in fact they seemed to make love just about every place
it was possible to—and a few others besides. They didn't
leave the flat all weekend, staying in bed to watch old
black and white films of which there was a vast col-

lection. They never, she realised afterwards, got around to swopping surnames, but they talked law and they talked politics. They discovered that neither of them could draw to save their lives, but they both loved chess—Elizabeth even beat him twice.

'Never been beaten by a woman before,' he said, with grudging admiration.

'Sexist!' she retorted.

He raised his hands in the air. 'But I'm usually the best.'

'Perhaps I'm better?'

He grinned. 'Then let's try and think of something *I'm* good at, shall we?'

There were several things he was *very* good at, she thought dreamily as she let him unbutton the oversized shirt of his she was wearing, and which she'd only just put on.

He kept sending out for treats she'd never had before— a champagne breakfast with a crimson rose lying on the tray; smoked salmon and bagels. Even oysters.

'They're supposed to be an aphrodisiac,' he told her, his eyes twinkling as he sprinkled one with raspberry vinegar before holding it up to her mouth.

'Then—do you think we should?' she enquired innocently, loving the way he laughed, the way he put the plate firmly away before taking her into his arms.

'You're going to be the death of me,' he murmured. 'Do you know that?'

'Am I?' she enquired breathlessly, holding her mouth up to be kissed. Or would it be vice versa? Didn't a part of her feel that she could curl up and die of pleasure, right then and there in his arms? She hadn't given a

thought to what was going to happen when the weekend
would end. She couldn't bear to think about it.

So she didn't.

But on the Sunday night she awoke in the early hours,
the space on the bed beside her empty. She lay in the
dimly lit silence, and then, as her eyes became used to
the light—she saw him. Standing with his back to her
on the balcony, a small white towel wrapped round him
which only barely covered the narrow hips, his stance
unmoving as he watched the pale fireworks of dawn begin
to gild the sky.

The set of his broad, bare shoulders made her aware
that something troubled him deeply—and she saw him
shake his head, heard a muttered, 'Damn!' and then,
'*Damn*!' again and she closed her eyes quickly as she
saw him start to move, afraid to look at him, to read
the regret in his eyes.

But he didn't come back to bed; instead he went in
the direction of one of the showers along the corridor—
presumably so as not to disturb her—but the sound of
the telephone did.

It had not rung all weekend and she picked it up, instinctively alert, wary, her heart in her mouth.

'Hello?' she said quietly.

A woman's voice; deep, husky, American. 'Is that the
maid?'

The *maid*! 'I——' stuttered Beth.

'Is Riccardo there?' butted in the voice impatiently.

'Not at the moment——' Elizabeth felt utterly lost,
like a fish floundering.

'Just who *is* that?' demanded the voice, authoritative
and very preppy, and its tone changed Cinderella back

again. She stopped being the young woman who had felt so loved and wanted in Riccardo's arms—and became Beth again, the girl whose mother hadn't wanted her, who had abandoned her in a cardboard box outside the police station. Beth, the girl from the orphanage.

'It's the maid,' she lied softly, without knowing why she said it.

'Oh. Well, have him call Brooke, will you?'

'Brooke?' she echoed stupidly.

'Yes, Brooke. His fiancée.'

Elizabeth stared steadily at the implacable features of Rick, her retreat into the past filling her with a new kind of strength. Yes, she could understand his anger at suddenly discovering that he was a father, and perhaps she had been wrong to conceal it from him, especially since his return. But he was not going to waltz back into her life and threaten everything that she had worked for.

Weren't they adults? Intelligent adults who could surely forge some mutually acceptable agreement between themselves concerning Peter? Because Elizabeth was certain of one thing—that Rick would be the last man to want to walk away from his son, now that he had discovered him—but where did that leave her?

'Mum! Mum! I've packed the picnic!' and Peter came dashing into the sitting-room, his young face alive with pleasure as his eyes darted quickly to Rick, as if checking that he was still there.

'That's great,' she said evenly. 'I'll just grab us some jackets, and then we'll go.'

Rick smiled down at Peter, and Elizabeth realised with a guilty flinch that it hurt to see the way her eight-year-old son positively glowed back. But apart from a couple of teachers at school, he didn't have much contact with males. No role models, she thought, immediately feeling guilty.

'Where would you most like to go, Peter?'

Peter's eyes were hopeful. 'Anywhere in the world?'

'Anywhere you like.'

'Can we—go to Thorpe Park?'

'You've got it!'

'*Great*! Thanks, Rick.' Peter was already tugging at the tall man's hand, Elizabeth observed as she followed them helplessly outside to where Rick's fire-engine-red car waited, watching as they walked side by side, the same long, loping stride, dark heads bent as they talked, already conspirators.

Thorpe Park, the giant theme park just outside London, was a huge success, with Peter going on every single ride he could. Elizabeth was torn between wanting to enjoy his obvious pleasure, and a feeling of resentment, that somehow, even though *she* had brought Peter here from time to time, Rick's presence was making it doubly enjoyable for him. For a start, he accompanied Peter on rides she wouldn't have gone *near*!

She found herself covertly watching the man, recognising that the once potent attraction she had felt for him had not relinquished its hold at all. A man who was also being openly stared at by other women at the theme park, in the same way that the waitress had ogled him in the bar. Mothers with young children unashamedly admired the strong lines of his body, and his dramatically dark good looks as he went laughingly on every terrifying ride with Peter. The man who had changed her life, unknowingly, perhaps uncaringly, but through her son their destinies were now firmly interlinked.

And he was so good with Peter—gentle and firm—yet fun. He had that way with children which all Italian men, even second and third generation ones, seemed to have. Of genuinely *liking* children, and respecting them, she thought—other people's, too. And yet it added to his masculinity rather than detracted from it.

She found herself on the one hand reluctantly admiring the way her boy warmed to the tall Italian whom he had yet to discover was his father, but even as she watched she shivered as she thought about that evening, nervous of the inevitable confrontation which was brewing in his eyes. He was playing a part with her now, for Peter's sake—being polite and friendly towards her—but a world away from real communication.

They got soaking wet on some of the rides and had the sandwiches they'd made for lunch, then ate massive hamburgers in the afternoon, washed down with strawberry milkshakes. Or rather, Peter and Rick did. Elizabeth just sat there, nibbling at little bits of the bun, but unable to try more than a morsel of the meat which grew steadily more inedible the colder it became.

Eventually, the day came to an end, much to Peter's disappointment, even though Elizabeth could see how tired he was.

'Where are we going now?' Peter asked eagerly, once the three of them were buckled into the large BMW.

'Home-time,' said Rick, his eyes meeting Elizabeth's over Peter's head.

'*Oh*!' protested Peter automatically.

'What's up?' asked Rick gently. 'There'll be other days.'

Peter scowled. 'I probably won't get to see you again.'

'Oh, you'll get to see me again. That I promise you.' Bright eyes lanced into her like a laser. 'You see, Peter, now that I've found you and your mother again, I intend to see you as much as I possibly can.'

CHAPTER FIVE

'THAT sounded very like a threat,' said Elizabeth, trying to keep the shakiness from her voice as he started up the car engine.

They had just dropped Peter off at home, and Elizabeth had quickly showered and changed from her jeans.

'A threat?' He turned towards her, but the fading light meant that all she could see was a harshly defined and shadowed face.

'About seeing a lot of us.' Thank God for the darkness, which meant that her own giveaway rise of colour went unnoticed.

He started the engine smoothly and shook his dark head. 'No, Elizabeth, not a threat. I've never yet threatened a woman, and I don't intend to start now. Look on it more as a promise, if you like.'

'A promise?'

'Yes, indeed. That now I've found my son, I don't intend to let him go easily.'

Her breath caught painfully in her throat, realising that her subconscious, at least, had wanted to hear something entirely different. She was a fool. Because when Rick had told Peter that he didn't intend to let her go, there had been an instinctive and heady rush of excitement as she had mistaken the meaning of his words. The message he had meant to convey was that he didn't

intend to let Peter go, but he could hardly tell the boy
that. So he had coated his words in conventionality and
had included her. And however much he denied it—that
did sound like a threat to her. A threat to her secure and
happy future.

She leaned back in her seat, staring down at her clasped
hands. Tonight, deliberately, she had dressed up, wearing
a short black silk dress with tiny pearl buttons up the
front from neck to thigh. Over it she wore a loose black
chiffon overshirt. Earrings and a necklace of jet glittered darkly at her throat and ears and she wore eye-
shadow, mascara *and* blusher—the whole works;
finishing off with a soft red lipstick which emphasised
the fullness of her mouth. She had stared back at her
image in her bedroom mirror, totally satisfied. Tonight,
with the sleek lines of her clothes and her gleaming,
golden-brown cap of hair, there was no trace of Beth
whatsoever. Tonight, she was elegant, assured Elizabeth.

Except that she was not; not really. Inwardly, she
dreaded the outcome of tonight's meal. Would he
threaten her with legal action? Or, worse still, try to
seduce her? To have her at his mercy both mentally *and*
physically?

He drove her to a restaurant near Holborn; she had
read all the rave reviews about it. It was neither osten-
tatious nor spartan, but Elizabeth felt it was a waste—
she might as well have eaten canteen food for all she
tasted it.

Ordering their food and wine at first meant that there
was no need for ordinary conversation, but, once the
waiter had left them with two glasses of Chablis and a

little dish of olives, a charged silence fell, and Elizabeth forced herself not to bow to the strength of his will.

'Don't you think,' she said, 'that it's a little hypo-critical of us to sit in a fancy restaurant pretending that we're discussing the weather——?'

'Instead of my son's welfare——'

'*Our* son's welfare,' she corrected bitterly. 'And don't you ever forget it.'

His eyes narrowed. 'That much you concede.'

The word stilled her. It was a lawyer's word, and the thought of concessions, of having to relinquish some-thing, anything, of her precious son, filled her with the light of battle and she felt a renewed rush of strength, as motherhood invested her with its own protective power. 'Let me tell you this, Rick,' she said in a voice which was as steady as a rock. 'That Peter is my son, and I love him. What is more, I have always cared for him. And I defy anyone to find an area in his life—physically or emotionally—where he is neglected.'

She leaned forward a fraction across the table, fixing her eyes on his and meeting that blue-green stare head on. 'Now I don't know what kind of pull fathers have in the States. I know you're a barrister and I know you're good—I've read your file. I also know you're rich—far richer than I will ever be—and I'm old enough to also know that money is power. But you *shan't* take Peter away from me—you just *shan't*! And what's more, I'll fight you in any court in the world to prove it—and if that fails I'll take him away, far away—where you'll never set eyes on either one of us again.' Her breathing was laboured as she came to the end of her impassioned little speech and she stared at him defiantly, expecting him to give back as good as he'd got—maybe more. But he watched her with icy calm, as though they already stood across a courtroom. She could see his thoughts ticking over carefully as he surveyed her, as dispassionately as if she'd been on the witness stand in front of him, his trained lawyer's mind never slipping into the hysteria he probably thought she had just been giving full rein to.

'You think that's what I'm intending to do?' he asked, and there was a tone in his voice which made her look up quickly. 'To take him away from you?'

Ridiculously, something in the way he asked the question filled her momentarily with guilt, but she vanquished the feeling immediately, looking at him full in the face, trying to ignore the bittersweet memories which those carved, handsome features provoked in her. 'I have no idea what you're intending to do,' she answered, equally quietly. 'Perhaps you'd like to tell me?'

His blue-green eyes caught the rays from the soft light which hung over their table—beautiful, disturbing eyes which still had the power to haunt her.

'It's too early to say,' he answered obliquely, studying her for a long moment, a piercing look in his eyes which had the effect of hardening his expression. 'How?' he asked at last.

She blinked, momentarily nonplussed. 'How what?'

'Peter,' he said impatiently. 'How did it happen? I made sure that I protected you.'

She felt wild colour scorch its path over her pale skin. To Elizabeth it felt like the ultimate in humiliation to sit here in this restaurant and discuss failed contraception in the cold light of day, nine years after the event.

'How?' he said again, very softly.

Oh, God. She found herself wanting to wring her hands, like a heroine in some awful melodrama. 'That time...there was that one time...during the night. I...we...don't you remember?' she finished at last, desperately.

There was a pause. She saw the momentary frown followed by a brief flare in the light eyes as he lifted his gaze to hers and nodded his head. 'Of course I remember.' There was a long pause. 'I thought it was a dream,' he said, in a strangely husky voice.

And so, too, at first, had she. That episode in the strangely unreal hours between night and day, when they had half-woken at the same time, sleepily reached for one another without knowing that they did so. It had been their own particular witching hour. Magical. For no *real* lovemaking could have been that perfect. Oh, the other times he had taken her that weekend had given them both the ultimate in mutual pleasure, but that episode had been a time out of mind. The slow, wordless coupling which had seemed to lift them out of their earthly confines, and on to another plane altogether...

'No dream,' she said flatly, remembering with stark horror the reality of her positive pregnancy test a fortnight later, though if she were really honest she had felt the change and the flowering in her body the very day after that extraordinary lovemaking. She remembered sitting in Donna's tiny bathroom, staring at the tiny test-tube in her shaking hand as she faced the thought of a future alone with her child...

'No dream,' she repeated.

'No.' He was staring at her very hard. 'What did you do?'

'What do you think I did?' she demanded. 'I had the baby.'

'But you had won a scholarship? To Oxford, wasn't it?'

She was half surprised he had remembered that. She nodded. 'Yes, a scholarship which was supposed to be the culmination of a life spent studying. I gave it up to have Peter,' she said brutally. 'I had no choice.'

But he shook his head. 'There is always——' he spoke with deliberation '—a choice.'

How ugly it sounded. She couldn't repress a shudder as she lifted her shoulders. 'Not for me,' she said proudly, her chin tipping up, the silky hair falling thickly onto her long neck.

'No?'

'Not for a minute, not even for a second.'

'You wanted a baby so much?'

Not a baby, *your* baby, she realised, but with realisation came the resentment, long and necessarily repressed. 'What do you think? Of *course* I didn't want a *baby*!' she said. 'Not then! I wanted to use my brains, I wanted to *go* to Oxford! I wanted the chance to compete with some of the finest brains in the country. I wanted to make something of myself...' With a trembling hand she reached for her glass and took a huge mouthful of wine, wishing that she hadn't exposed herself with that pathetic little display of self-pity, when his next words rocked her.

'But you *have* succeeded. You *have* made something of yourself,' he pointed out. 'And Peter is a wonderful child—a credit to you.'

She eyed him suspiciously, waiting for the inevitable barb, but none came, and his remark demanded courtesy. 'Thank you,' she said, a little stiffly.

'And you married—quite soon—afterwards?'

'Yes.' Would he never let up?

'And did you love him, Elizabeth?' A strange, watchful light glowed at the back of his eyes as he asked the question.

He had no right to ask, not after what he had done to her. She studied the untouched roll on her side-plate. John had been a kind, wonderful man. He had given her so much at a time when she really needed it. She would be forever indebted to him. 'I'm not answering any questions about John,' she said, with a quiet dignity. It was not a question she could properly answer, in any case. Oh, she had loved John, yes—in a way. But love was such an all-encompassing word—what she had felt for John hadn't at all resembled what she'd felt for Rick, and she had been certain that she loved *him*. And yet how could she have loved a man who could use her so thoroughly, betray her without compunction?

She looked up gratefully to see that the waiter had brought their Caesar salads, staring down at the coddled egg which gilded the lettuce leaves as though it were the single most fascinating thing in the world.

They ate the remainder of the meal mostly in a tense kind of silence, or rather, Rick did. Elizabeth ate very little, but she sipped at her wine as if it was going out of fashion, though so sombre was her mood that nothing could lift it, not even wine, and she ended up with a headache, and refused both cheese and pudding.

The waiter brought a coffee-pot to their table and with a small movement of his hand Rick indicated that he should leave them.

He leaned forward. 'Tell me how you like your coffee.'

'Black, no sugar, please.' She gave a low, humourless laugh. 'How little we really know of each other,' she said bitterly.

'You think so? And yet we are parents.'

'A biological accident,' she said, hating herself as she spoke the truth, knowing how it would upset Peter if he could hear her words. And then Rick's words seemed to uncannily echo her thoughts.

'What have you told Peter?' he asked harshly. 'Does he know anything about his real father? Or did he grow up believing that your *husband* had fathered him?'

She froze him with a stare. 'I've never once—*once*— lied to Peter. I told him the truth—or as much of it as I thought a young boy should know.'

'That being?'

Pointless to admit that she had told Peter of the deep love she'd had for his father. Messy admissions of her emotional attachment would only complicate an issue which needed to be sorted out with sense and logic. 'I told him that very often—relationships—don't—work out, and that his—father—had long since disappeared from our lives.'

He brought his cup down heavily onto the saucer, but the delicate porcelain withstood the assault. 'Did you tell him that I was given no choice? That I was kept in the dark about his very existence?'

But she *had* tried to contact him; she'd felt that he had a right to know about the baby, and perhaps she had fostered some small hope that he might want her if there was a baby... She had spoken to his aunt—but his aunt had obviously never told him.

She stared up into his starkly handsome face as she remembered. He doesn't *deserve* to know, she thought fiercely as the memories of that awful day came rushing back.

She remembered how low she had felt as she had rung on the door of his uncle's flat and an elegant blonde woman in her middle to late forties, dressed from head to toe in couture clothes, had looked down her nose at her with icy blue eyes. 'Yes?' she had enquired doubtfully, in a faint mid-Atlantic accent.

'You're Riccardo's aunt?' guessed Beth, nervously moistening her mouth.

Two arched and plucked eyebrows disappeared into hair of palest ash. 'And who might you be?' she returned.

'I'm Beth. Is—is—Riccardo here?' Beth had asked, and perhaps her desperation had showed.

'Riccardo? No, I'm afraid he isn't.' And then the woman had peered closely at Beth's white face, the red-rimmed and tear-stained eyes, and had given a little laugh. 'Oh, dear me—not *another* one!' She shook her head from side to side, but the ash blonde hair didn't move an inch. 'Wherever he goes, the little girls run after him.' She gave what Beth supposed was a helpful smile. 'Let me give you a word of advice—Beth, wasn't it? Do yourself a favour, and forget him, huh?'

But Beth thought of their baby and stuck to her guns. 'Did he leave a forwarding address?' she persisted.

A frown creased the stretched white forehead. 'Don't you understand, dear?' she asked gently. 'He's getting married. To Brooke.'

And after that Beth hadn't been able to pretend that Brooke hadn't been important. She had taken the only opportunity open to her and run out sobbing into the street. She had made her way to Hyde Park and had sat on a bench crying and crying, for what seemed like hours.

But when all her tears had been spent, she had risen slowly from the bench, a new resolve filling her with inner strength.

She knew what she had to do.

For a brief second she let her hand lie over her flat stomach, and made a silent promise to this child who had already been deserted, just as *she* had once been deserted by her mother. I'll protect you, she vowed. Whatever it takes, I'll protect you.

She had found a room quite easily, a scruffy room, true, but a room all the same. And then a job, as clerk to an accountant.

John had been her boss, a quiet, kind, diffident man who had had problems of his own. Years of caring for an invalid mother had meant that he had missed out on marriage and now that his mother had died he was, so he told her, desperately lonely, with his own particular cross to bear. It was a cross which made Beth's own particular 'problem' seem almost a gift. For while she was in the process of creating a new life, John was fighting to save his own from a newly diagnosed and fatal disease.

And by the end of a few weeks, he had convinced her that he could provide the security she needed while she could provide something this dying man's money couldn't buy—a child. And Beth had agreed to marry him.

Elizabeth came back to the present to find herself staring up at Rick's impassive features, realising that none of the whole awkward business had been sorted out.

'Tell me what it is that you want,' she asked expressionlessly.

He knew, it appeared, exactly what he wanted. 'I want the chance to see Peter, to get to know him.'

She let out a sigh. It was no less than she had expected. 'For how long?'

'While I am here in England—a few months, at most.'

'And then?'

He began to rise from the chair. 'That is, I think, a question which is unanswerable. For now.'

'And when would you want to see him? After school? With me?'

She hated having to ask it, but she had to know.

'Whenever fits in with his schoolwork and his hobbies. And no, not with you. I would prefer to see him alone. You, Elizabeth, remain a distraction.' And he stood up.

She knitted her eyebrows together as another problem came into focus. 'I don't know what I'm going to tell Peter—about you.'

'Say nothing for the time being. A big declaration isn't needed. Let him learn to know me, and to trust me. He may guess.' He saw her face. 'Yes, *guess*. Children know a good deal more than we give them credit for.'

'Perhaps you're right.'

He paid the bill and they left the restaurant, driving swiftly to her house, where he took her keys from her, but she shrank back as he opened the front door and let her precede him. He was too big and much, much too close for comfort.

He must have seen her small shiver, for his mouth twisted into a hard line. He was within touching distance and she could almost feel the tension, like an unwelcome predator, eating away at her nerve-endings.

He gave a harsh little laugh. 'Yes, it's tempting, isn't it, Elizabeth?' his voice lowered, yet his words were not provocative, simply matter-of-fact. 'You feel it too. We both feel it, even after all this time. To know that we are alone, that upstairs is a bed, and that nothing is stopping us from going to lie down on it. Perhaps it would do something to rid us of the bad blood which lies between us. Mmm? What do you say, Elizabeth?'

Dimly, she realised that he was shutting the front door behind him and pushing her into the sitting-room and that she was moving to order, like a puppet whose strings he was pulling.

She knew what he was about to do, knew that she should be saying no to him, but the words would not come. She watched him lock the door and still she did nothing. She stood there, like a stranger in her own home while he lit two lamps and she stood staring at him, her mouth dry as parchment, her heart thundering like the sound of a waterfall, so loud that she was surprised he didn't hear it.

His eyes were dark as the night, and a small smile played at the corner of his mouth as he came towards her until there were only inches between them.

He lifted up a hand to touch the side of her face, framed it there for a second so that she breathed in and then let the breath out on a deep sigh of anticipation as he let the hand trail further down, fingertips touching her neck, her shoulder, until at last he reached his destination and cupped the mound of her breast, his fingers finding her nipple with possessive skill.

He must have heard the sigh, for the smile deepened and, one hand still teasing her nipple into rock-hard ecstasy, his other hand snaked round her waist, and he pushed her to the ground.

Reason would have stopped her, but the desires he was reawakening in her ruthlessly refused to listen to something as mundane as reason.

Shamelessly she let him push her gently down until she was lying like a siren on the Persian rug, with Rick crouched beside her. She sighed again.

'I know,' he said. 'I know.'

She shut her eyes; his voice held a strangely abrasive quality which she had no wish to see for fear that it would destroy the insidiously powerful longings which held her body in silken thrall.

He pushed the dark gauze of the overshirt away and began to unbutton the black silk dress, all the way down.

'Did you wear this knowing that I was going to take it off?' he murmured, in a velvet voice.

'I——' Well, had she? Even subconsciously?

All the buttons undone, he pushed both halves of the silky fabric aside, not moving, not saying anything for a moment.

She opened her eyes quickly to see what was wrong and encountered a look of naked desire as he feasted his eyes on her partially clothed body. A look which terrified and yet thrilled her to the deepest, darkest core of her body.

His palms circled slowly over the black lace of the frivolous little bra, and Elizabeth closed her eyes again, her hips moving in the same age-old rhythm as she felt a shudderingly primitive warmth at the apex of her thighs.

He reached out to deftly unclip the front fastening of her bra, and when he had done so her breasts spilled out—joyously unrestrained—aching and tender and exquisitely aroused.

Oh, please, she begged silently, and, as if he'd heard her, he bent his dark head to clamp the warmth of his mouth possessively over one sensitive nub.

She gave a little cry as he licked her there, gently bit at her, until she thought that she would die.

The aching deep within her grew even more intense, and perhaps she communicated this to him, too, for his free hand moved slowly and inexorably to her panties.

'*Oh!*' she gasped, as he ruthlessly pushed the lace aside to let his fingers slide in to touch her with longed-for intimacy.

And once he had made contact with the acutely sensitised flesh, she knew that it was too late to stop him.

This was a dream; a precious, beautiful, erotic dream. This was Riccardo, after all—her darling, beloved Riccardo, who could bring her to complete and utter fulfilment.

Sweat broke out in tiny beads on her forehead as she called out his name, her hands clutching at the dark head which still suckled her breast even while his fingers worked their wilful magic.

Too late she felt the tide welling. She wanted him, she needed him, deep within her.

'I know,' he murmured again. 'Believe me, I know.'

He *couldn't* know! Because the tide was welling, on a crest now, and if he didn't stop what he was doing...

The sound of the mighty grandfather clock chiming midnight broke into her ectastic state like an invader, forcing her unwillingly back to reality. Just for a second she opened her hooded eyes and met his smoky gaze as he lifted his head from her breast. His look was impenetrable, with an indecipherable flicker which was gone in an instant as he levered himself away from her.

Appalled, she saw herself through his eyes—stockinged legs still bent, her dress pushed aside, her bra half-off and a telltale rosy flush all over her.

'You'd better do your dress up,' he said harshly, and he stood up suddenly, the line of his shoulders very rigid.

She lay unmoving, too shaken to do anything other than stare up at him.

'For God's sake! Do it up! *Now!*' But his voice held a strange catch to it.

With trembling fingers she did as he ordered, and, as what had just happened dwindled into a bitter memory, a shameful secret, she met his eyes with fury as she staggered to her feet. She could see how aroused he was and she knew that, with such a willing partner, most men would not have stopped then, would have gone on to have made love. But Rick was not, she realised bitterly, most men.

He must have seen the look in her eyes for he nodded grimly. 'Oh, yes, Elizabeth—I want you, make no mistake about that. The temptation to carry you up those stairs and spend the rest of the night making love to you is almost as powerful as the life-force itself. We could climb naked beneath the sheets and make love and maybe that could make us forget all the deceit, all the wasted years.'

'Wasted years?' The words stumbled out, her heart leaping with a naïve hope which seemed to spring from nowhere.

But he moved back to the door and unlocked it, his face fierce with dark anger. 'Yes, wasted years. Without my son. You've denied me eight years of my son's life, Elizabeth—and for that I don't think I'll ever forgive you.'

She blanched at the raw derision in his voice.

'Just get out of here!' she hissed between gritted teeth.

'Oh, don't worry, honey—I'm going!'

And he slammed out, leaving Elizabeth standing trembling against the door for support, her eyes closed as tears began to slide slowly down her face.

Oh, lord—what had she *done*? How could she have behaved like that? How could she have let him...let him...? She shuddered, her shame removing the last traces of passion, and silently she crept upstairs to take the longest shower of her life.

CHAPTER SIX

ELIZABETH put down the receiver with a shaking hand.

She had just confirmed with Rick that he would collect Peter at two that afternoon, to take him to a children's theatre.

He had started seeing his son once or twice a week. It was bizarre, crazy—and she could hardly believe it was happening.

Not that it had all gone smoothly. On the first occasion Rick had called round, Peter had shown a surprising reluctance to go on an outing alone with him, and without his mother.

Though perhaps it wasn't really very surprising, she thought. The atmosphere between the two of them was so understandably strained that the child was probably thoroughly bewildered.

The first time that she'd seen Rick after that disgraceful episode on the floor of her sitting-room, she hadn't felt like looking him in the eye. But pride and indignation refused to let her cower like a beaten dog. *He*, after all, had been the one to ruthlessly manipulate her body using his skilful but heartless lovemaking techniques. And her body had been too long neglected to do anything other than rocket crazily out of control.

She had spent sleepless nights shamefully reliving it, until, one morning in the early hours, she had thought *damn* him! And if he wanted to see her all vulnerable and apologetic, then he would have a long wait! So she opened the door to him with a defiant spark in her eyes, and she saw something very like humour sparking in his.

He turned to Peter. 'Ready to go?' he asked, in his deep, drawling voice.

'I don't want to go,' said Peter stubbornly. 'Not without Mummy.'

The situation was easily remedied.

'You'll come with us today, won't you, Elizabeth?' The light eyes were turned on her in question. She was trapped. Of course she didn't want to go. But what could she do? 'I'll come this once,' she said reluctantly.

But gradually, over a few weeks, Rick wore Peter down. With love, Elizabeth realised, hating herself for the pang of resentment she experienced, hating herself more when she analysed it, knowing that she was actually feeling a little jealous of her own son.

She resisted the urge to interrogate Peter on his return from each day's outings, but sometimes the temptation proved too much.

'What do you and Rick talk about?' she asked over breakfast one Sunday morning, while they were waiting for him to call to take Peter to Madame Tussaud's.

Peter slapped two inches of strawberry jam on to a slice of toast. 'Oh, you know,' he answered vaguely.

'I *don't* know,' said Elizabeth testily. 'That's why I'm asking.'

Peter shrugged, finished chewing a mouthful of toast and jam and looked up at her. 'Well, when we go to the zoo, we talk about all the animals, where they come from, what they're descended from. He's seen real lions, you know, in the wild. And cheetah. When he was at university—he went to Africa and made a film about them.'

Which is more than I knew, thought Elizabeth. 'But does he ever talk about his life in America? His family there?'

'It's not a very big family, I think,' said Peter doubtfully, chewing his lip in the way he always did when he felt uncomfortable.

'How big?'

'I don't know. Why don't you ask him?'

'Because I don't *want* to ask him,' said Elizabeth crossly.

'Well, *I'll* ask him, then, shall I?'

'Don't you *dare*!'

She realised that she and Rick were behaving like a newly divorced couple. By silent and mutual consent, they behaved impeccably towards each other in front of Peter. The polite if frosty handover of child to man on the doorstep, the meaningless little interchanges about the weather. Which actually hurt much more than it should have done. But perhaps that was the only way. It meant that Rick could build a relationship with his son, without the flashpoint of emotions, like a chemical reaction, which always seemed to occur when the two of *them* got together for more than two minutes.

And at the same time as he was deepening his relationship with Peter, Rick was setting up his chambers with what, to Elizabeth, seemed like astonishing speed and efficiency.

At the office no one, apart from Jenny, knew that Rick had been visiting her house to collect Peter regularly. She tried to imagine Paul's face if she had suddenly announced that she was the mother of Rick Masterton's child!

One day, Rick had insisted on making an appointment with her, and just before he was due to arrive, Paul came in to discuss a client with her.

After she had succinctly recited the facts, she looked up into Paul Meredith's handsome face. 'I can't figure out exactly *why* Rick Masterton is bothering to open up chambers in England,' she said. 'Not when it's costing him a fortune.'

Paul shrugged. 'He can afford it. Plus he's bringing a lot of American clients with him. Besides, he likes to diversify.' He hesitated. 'There's more than one rumour that says he's thinking of running for public office.' He laughed. 'Can't you see Rick as president of the USA one day?'

That was just the trouble—she *could*! He had everything that a candidate could possibly want—a first class academic record, the ability to use the power of persuasive logic gained during his legal career—oh, and charisma. Certainly charisma—he had enough of that to sink a battle ship.

When Jenny buzzed through to announce his arrival, she automatically murmured to usher him in, quite used to his presence due to his frequent visits to Peter—but still her heart hammered like crazy in her ribcage.

But she was unprepared for the distinctly hostile flash in his eyes, and as he came in she realised that Paul had been leaning over her chair, one arm draped casually along the back.

A strangely satisfying buzz fizzed through her. Surely, surely—Rick wasn't *jealous*? But then he stepped forward, his hand extended, his eyes crinkling at the corners as he smiled.

'Paul,' he said warmly, and then she knew that she must have imagined it. Jealous? Why on earth would he be jealous? He'd already told her bitterly that he didn't think he'd ever forgive her for keeping Peter's birth a secret.

What *had* surprised her more than anything was that Peter accepted Rick's new and apparently fixed role in his life, without questioning it.

Or so she thought. But the following evening, when Rick was dropping him off after an exhausting day at the seaside, the boy had looked up at Elizabeth, his eyes shining.

'Can't Daddy stay for supper tonight?'

There was a complete and breathless silence. Elizabeth looked directly at Rick, saw that he had recovered his composure far more quickly than her, but the look in his eyes told her that he was leaving it to her to take the lead.

'What did you call Rick?' she asked quietly.

Peter looked from one adult to the other. Then went red. 'Daddy,' he mumbled, then lifted a defiant gaze in which Elizabeth saw herself so clearly that it made her heart melt. 'Well, he is my daddy, isn't he?'

Elizabeth's pupils contracted under the direct glare of Rick's gaze. She remembered telling him how she'd never lied to Peter. 'Yes, darling,' she said quietly. 'He is. How—how did you guess?'

'He looks like me. But it's more than that—he just *knows* me.' The curl of the small mouth was belligerent, the question accusing as he turned his gaze on Rick. 'Why did you never come to see me before?'

Elizabeth could have wept at the solemn little query. She bit her lip, unable to answer, awaiting the harsh facts to be recounted by Rick.

But he surprised her with his soft tone. 'Because Mummy and Daddy lost touch with each other a long time ago.'

'How long?'

'Before you were born.'

Elizabeth's eyes sent him a beseeching look. You couldn't expect a child of eight to cope with the reality of their passionate fling.

And, to her relief, he obviously agreed. 'It's too difficult to explain it all to you now, Peter.' He put one hand on to Peter's shoulder. 'The things that grown-ups do are very complicated sometimes. The most important thing is that we've found one another again——'

'And you're not going away again?'

There was an awkward silence. Peter looked up, his eyes overbright. 'You *are*, aren't you? You'll go away again and I'll never see you again, and I won't have a father again. I *hate* you!'

He ran from the room and Elizabeth made to move after him.

'Leave him.'

Tears were brimming in her own eyes. 'I must go to him——'

He shook his head. 'Give him a few minutes. Let him cry.'

'What good has come of all this?' she demanded bitterly. 'We've ended up by hurting Peter more than if he'd never known of your existence——'

He shook his head. 'That isn't true, and you know it,' he said flatly. 'Peter has merely brought to a head something which we would have had to face sooner or later. I don't want to lose touch with him again, Elizabeth. Ever. Do you understand that?'

Yes, she understood, and, standing there under the direct scrutiny of his stare, she understood something else, too. Why the whole situation was more fraught than it need have been. If only she had done the sensible thing and found someone else in the intervening years. If only she could have fallen in love with another man. Then, she could have seen Rick in his correct and only role—as Peter's father.

But instead, he confused and overwhelmed her, because the feelings for him which she'd always had—feelings which had caused her to behave totally out of character—those feelings had never really gone away. Still, he aroused in her a yearning to be near him. She wanted him to respect her, to like her. And physically, she still wanted him just as badly as she had done as an unawakened girl of eighteen...

She forced herself to be rational. 'What happens when you go back to the States?'

'I wanted to talk to you about that in any case. I've almost tied up the ends here. The business is ready to roll—I don't need to come back for at least six months. You know that.'

With a huge effort, she became his accountant for a moment. 'Yes, I know,' she said heavily. 'As long as you're back some time in March, just before our tax year ends.'

He nodded, pushing his hands down deep into the pockets of his dark cords, the thick material doing nothing to disguise the sheer power which lay tensed beneath the strong shaft of his thighs. 'It won't be long until July,' he continued in that neutral voice, as though it wasn't her son's future he was discussing so calmly. 'The long vacation starts soon. I'd like to take Peter home with me for a holiday, if you're agreeable.'

Panic set in; she found herself clutching the back of a chair for support. The seven long weeks of the summer holidays. She imagined Peter lured away by this rich and glamorous man he had quickly grown to love—to a lotus land of sunshine and swimming-pools.

'No, Rick,' she said, with quiet determination. 'I can't let you do that, I just can't. Not take Peter out of the country.'

His voice was equally quiet. 'You don't trust me? You don't think I'll return him?'

But strangely enough, it wasn't that at all. She didn't know how much he valued women, but she had a strong hunch about how much he valued his son. 'I trust you,' she said slowly, and heard him mutter something softly underneath his breath. 'But I'm afraid to let him go.' Afraid he won't want to come back. 'We've never been apart before and I'll miss him,' she said tremulously. 'Don't you understand that?'

The light eyes narrowed and he frowned, about to speak.

'Can't Mum come too?' asked a voice at the door, and they both whirled round—Elizabeth astonished to see that Peter's tears had dried, that he appeared calm, apart from the occasional sniff and that he was staring up openly into his father's face. 'Can't she?'

Rick's features showed not one flicker of emotion. 'If that is what you both decide you want, then of course she can come.'

But she could tell from his tone that it was not what he would have wanted, and inside Elizabeth crumbled like a water biscuit. If only he had shown *something*. For if he'd been vehemently opposed to her going, then at least she would have been justified in trying to stop Peter. Or if he'd been overjoyed? mocked a cruel inner voice. Wouldn't that have been the ideal scenario? The answer to all the fairy-stories?

She ran her fingers back through her hair in the way she always did when she was fraught. 'I don't know what to say,' she said, knowing that in this case there *was* no easy answer, no perfect solution. 'Do we have to decide anything tonight? I mean—why go back to the States, Rick? What's to stop you spending the summer here?'

'Because I too have other commitments——'

'He means my sister——' broke in Peter suddenly, and Elizabeth saw Rick frown at him.

The world spun on its axis. 'You mean—we've got a daughter?' she asked stupidly.

'*I* have a daughter,' he corrected, almost gently.

She focused on the door-handle, staring at it as though her life depended on it, trying to stop herself from asking the question which had suddenly become of paramount importance, the question whose answer she instinctively knew would smite another blow at her already badly beaten heart. But she had to know. 'How old is she?'

He hesitated, as if sensing the time-bomb which was about to explode. 'She's about the same age as Peter,' he said finally.

Elizabeth felt sick, her humiliation complete. 'And you *knew* that?' she asked Peter, his silent collusion on the matter seeming to strike the final nail in the coffin.

'But I *tried* to tell you, Mum,' he protested. 'And you said you didn't want to know.'

Rick said nothing but stood watching her every reaction, his eyes glittering.

Elizabeth cleared her throat, longing for this torture to be over. 'Then obviously the matter is decided. I am unwilling to let Peter travel without me, but naturally we couldn't presume to land ourselves on your family. Your wife...' God—his *wife*! It took every ounce of will she had not to let her voice break into a scream on that single word. 'I'm sure your wife wouldn't want your——'

'Before you go any further, Elizabeth. I have to tell you that my wife is dead. She died in a sailing accident six years ago.'

CHAPTER SEVEN

'DRINK this.'

Rick had come back from putting Peter to bed to find Elizabeth still sitting in a trance on the sofa. He took one look at her and strode straight over to the drinks cabinet. Elizabeth took the tumblerful of whisky mixed with water which he handed to her and drank off half of it in a single swallow.

He raised an eyebrow. 'Steady.'

The drink warmed her stomach instantly. In a way, the events of the evening had freed her. Nothing worse could possibly happen to her now. She felt her confidence return, she even managed to curve her lips into a smile.

'There's no need for you to play nursemaid. I've never yet had to resort to alcohol to get me out of a tight spot—and I certainly don't intend to start now.'

His mouth set into a hard line as he set his own glass down on the table in front of him. 'That's how you see it, is it? As a tight spot?'

Her glass joined his as she sat up straight and stared at him. 'Well, just how would you describe it? A red letter day? My son's father appears from out of the blue in the guise of a conquering hero who would appeal to any small boy. And now we discover that he has a stepsister—conveniently of the same age.' Her mouth curled in distaste. 'Handy for playtime,' she observed, her voice

dripping with sarcasm. 'But we might have a little trouble
explaining the timescale in years to come.' She picked
up her glass and swallowed some more whisky, the spirit
giving her the confidence to ask the dreaded question.
'What was your wife's name, by the way?'

She saw his eyes narrow. 'Brooke.'

'Brooke,' she mused, her words only slightly un-
steady, not giving a single thing away. Let the two-timing
rat stay ignorant of the fact she'd known that all along.
'What a very understanding woman she must have been.
Didn't she mind that you were out getting two women
pregnant simultaneously——?'

'Damn you, Beth!' he interrupted heavily, his voice
quiet enough not to wake Peter, but the softness of his
tone somehow only emphasised the violence of the ex-
pletive. 'What right do you have to play the role of high-
minded moral saviour? You couldn't wait to leave my
arms and marry the richest guy you could lay your hands
on; it didn't seem to matter that he was old enough to
be your bloody *father*! Tell me——' his eyes flicked ex-
pressive distaste over the length of her body '—how did
it feel to be bought, hmm?'

She went white. 'How *dare* you?'

'Oh, I dare all right. Tell me, Elizabeth, I want to
know. Tell me all about your marriage.'

'I'm not telling you anything,' she spat out. 'Because
it's none of your business.'

He fixed her with a glare she was sure could have in-
timidated anyone else. But not her. Oh, no. Not her.

'I'm making it my business,' he grated. 'He was, after
all, father to my son—while he was alive. But your face

never seems to light up when you talk of him. Although maybe that isn't so very surprising...'

She met his gaze steadily. 'Oh? And why's that?'

'Perhaps your attitude insulted him. Maybe he resented being taken for a ride by a—gold-digger—if you'll excuse the cliché?' he queried softly.

She gave him a chilly smile. 'Make your mind up, Rick,' she said coolly. 'First you accuse John and me of making the oldest barter of all time, namely, my youth in exchange for his money. Yet now you're suggesting that he *resented* my so-called "gold-digging" aspirations. You really will have to do better than that,' she said scornfully. 'Not a lot of lawyer's logic applied to *that* particular argument.'

A pulse worked furiously in his cheek. 'Maybe that's because I find it damn near impossible to use *any* kind of logic around *you!*' he snarled, and the look of fury on his face was such that she actually backed down.

'Just for the record,' she added quietly, 'I didn't marry him for his money.'

'Oh, really?' he mocked.

She nearly told him then. That she'd spoken to Brooke, and his aunt, how finding out that he had betrayed her had driven her into the security of John's arms—but why feed his ego? Let it remain a secret; her secret. It was a weapon she might be able to use against him.

He surveyed her unblinkingly, his arrogantly handsome face still set in those cold, hard lines. 'You still don't seem to have decided whether or not you're coming to America with Peter. I assume you *are* going to let him come?'

She gave a hollow laugh, wishing that she could do something to shake his composure. 'Naturally. He's desperate to go, and I'm not really willing to be cast in the role of wicked mother yet. God knows, I have trouble enough competing with you as it is.'

'It doesn't have to be a competition, Elizabeth.'

Her eyes flashed. 'No? The situation's impossible—I do know that.'

He gave a small shrug, as though he couldn't really care. 'Enough procrastination—are you coming to America as well, or not?'

'Once again, I seem to have no choice. Yes, of course I'll come.'

'There won't be a problem with work? With getting seven weeks off at once?'

'I'll speak to Paul. I'll have to employ a locum.'

'If you like I could always have a quiet word with Paul.'

'Just you try it, Rick.' She froze him with a stare. 'At work I'm my own woman, and I don't need any assistance from you. Now——' she put her half-full glass of whisky down on the table, suddenly sick of the stale taste of the spirit '—you'd better tell me what I'll expect to find when I get there.'

He took another sip of his scotch. 'My daughter,' he hesitated. 'Jessie.'

It was strange how much it should hurt. 'And who looks after—Jessie—while you're not there?'

'I have a housekeeper, and my mother lives nearby. Oh, and Grace.' He gave a small frown. 'She's round sometimes—not very often. That's Brooke's mother.'

'I see. And how do you suppose they are going to feel about Peter? Your son just sprung on them out of the blue?'

'I've already spoken to my mother on the phone. I'm flying ahead the weekend before so that I can have some time to get Jessie used to the idea. Then I'll fly back to accompany you both.' He paused. 'I think it's going to make it very difficult for everyone concerned if we continue to fight the way we have been doing.'

Her face was disbelieving. In the circumstances, just what did he expect? 'What are you suggesting? That we masquerade as best friends?'

He gave her a long, steady look. 'I'm suggesting that, in front of other people, at least—we could try being polite to one another. Do you think we could do that, Elizabeth? Who knows?' His voice became dry. 'It could become a habit.'

She doubted it, but she nodded reluctantly, knowing that he spoke sense. She and Peter would be the outsiders, and she the usurper—of Brooke's memory as wife and mother, and she needed Rick on her side. His mother would probably despise her, but she dreaded to think how Grace—Brooke's mother—would react to her presence, especially with Peter in tow—a living monument to Rick's infidelity.

She sighed, her eyes fixed on her lap, unwilling to be caught up in that searching look of Rick's, knowing that all her problems were made much worse by the fact that she still felt so strongly about the man who had fathered her child. How easy it would be if she could just disregard him, or, even better, be his friend—in the same way that so many people claimed to feel about their ex-spouses.

But there was something unresolved in their relationship—something which made her wary of staying with him, because it wasn't that she didn't trust *him*—more that she didn't trust her own response where this man was concerned. Look at the way she'd been that night he'd taken her out for dinner.

'Perhaps it would be better if Peter and I stayed nearby, but not at your home itself——'

'No.' He interrupted her with firm conviction. 'The complex is massive and there is room enough for us all to live there without falling over each other. But I want Peter to feel that it is *his* home, too. To get to know Jessie, and his grandparents.'

In a way he was right. 'He's always been a little short on relatives,' said Elizabeth, and a great sadness overwhelmed her for a moment. 'His legacy; and mine.'

'I know that, Beth,' he said softly.

When he was understanding like this, soft, kind, almost gentle, it was the cruellest cut of all. It let her imagination concoct foolish little fantasies of how easy it would be, how natural and how wonderful, if they could all be a family together.

But he betrayed you, reminded a voice. Betrayed you *and* the woman he married. And since he has been back, he has shown little inclination to do anything other than to berate you, or, occasionally, to demonstrate his sensual domination.

'So shall we try being polite to one another?' he prompted.

She knew it made sense, but he'd hurt her too much for her to give in too easily. 'If that's what you want.'

He gave a strange, empty laugh. 'Oh, I think we'll discount what it is *I* want. Somehow I don't much think you'd care to hear what that is.'

She didn't doubt him for a moment.

CHAPTER EIGHT

'I'M SURPRISED that you haven't chartered your own jet,' joked Elizabeth weakly as she accepted the glass of champagne which the stewardess offered her, surprised to *find* herself being light-hearted with Rick for the first time. And if she were being perfectly honest it was almost a relief to be able to relax enough to make a joke after the weeks of strain and sniping. But she had thought over what he'd said, and had decided that a truce would be easier to live with than all-out warfare—for Peter's sake, if for no one else's.

Broad shoulders, clad casually in soft peacock-green cashmere which reminded her of the younger man she had once known, were lifted in a careless shrug. 'I often hire planes,' he stated without boast, as matter-of-factly as she might have said, 'I often take the bus'. 'But for a transatlantic trip, I prefer the comfort of a scheduled flight.'

Elizabeth looked around the cabin, at its discreet luxury. She would hardly describe Concorde as 'just a scheduled flight'!

'What time do we land in New York?'

'We get into Kennedy at around eleven. A car will meet us there.'

'Oh,' said Elizabeth, rather faintly. This journey was in danger of letting her believe she was some kind of minor celebrity!

She watched as he turned to accept a glass of champagne from the stewardess, and gave her a delicious grin, and Elizabeth couldn't help noticing that, naturally, the blonde stewardess revealed a brilliant white smile to match his. This could be a match made in an orthodontist's heaven, thought Elizabeth nastily as she heard with resignation the furious pitter-pat of her heart which such a devastating smile produced, even if it *was* second-hand. He doesn't smile at *me* like that, she thought resentfully.

His eyes had narrowed as he studied her interest in her surroundings. 'Anyway—surely you had the luxury of travelling like this with your husband?' he continued in his deep, drawling voice, though the blue-green eyes were glacial. 'Supersonic jets, sumptuous yachts, the best hotels—these are all the hallmarks of the trophy wife, are they not?'

Elizabeth glanced quickly down at the slumped head of her sleeping son, worn out with excitement over this forthcoming trip. So that, then, was the reason why Rick was back to being as objectionable to her as possible—Peter had fallen asleep and was dead to the world. She looked up into that coldly handsome face, her fingers drawing stripes in the condensation which had formed on the outside of her champagne glass.

'This is the first time I've ever flown,' she told him.

He raised his eyebrows. 'Really? That must have been rather disappointing for you.'

Again, the implication that it had been the spoils which had been her main interest in the marriage. 'What would you say,' she asked slowly, 'if I told you again that I didn't marry John for his money?'

He gave the most cynical smile she had ever seen in her life. 'Oh, I stopped believing in fairy-tales a long time ago.'

She swallowed the lump in her throat. 'No, I'd like to know,' she persisted, as she heard the icy distaste in his voice. 'Really, I would.'

Again that mocking smile. 'I would say, my dear Elizabeth,' he said, very softly, for her ears only, 'that you were a beautiful but unconvincing liar.'

'Everything's that black and white for you, is it?' she said bitterly.

He shrugged, before fixing her with a penetrating stare that sent a shiver right down to the base of her spine. 'Then enlighten me, do. What was it—physical attraction?' he said sarcastically.

She acknowledged the barb. John had been small and bespectacled. A fine businessman, but an insignificant-looking man. It had not mattered to Beth—she had not been searching for physical attraction. At the time she had felt she'd had enough of that with Rick to last her a lifetime. Physical attraction got you into trouble and besides, she had believed that a physical relationship between herself and John would grow naturally out of a deep and mutual affection.

All the world saw was a nubile young woman, her arm linked with a bespectacled balding man, whose eyes already contained the secret of his impending death. But John had given her a chance to make something of herself, had loved her unequivocally.

'I *did* love John,' she said slowly. Maybe not in the way that she had loved Rick, but in a wholly intellectual and companionable sense. He was the father I never had, she realised, with a sudden flash of insight.

But, confusingly, instead of vindicating her, her words seemed to have had exactly the opposite effect. Rick's face had darkened. His anger was almost palpable; she could feel waves of it emanating from him, enveloping her, sweeping over her inexorably. 'So tell me,' he continued. 'Was he an "understanding" man, Elizabeth?'

She put her glass of champagne down on the table before her with shaking fingers. 'What's that supposed to mean?'

'Did he know about your little "flings"? Was your own relationship somewhat—lacking—in that department? Is that why you turned so eagerly to me?' His voice dropped to a mere whisper. 'You were the most passionate woman I've ever had in my bed, Elizabeth—before or since. I think I now know why.'

'You are disgusting,' she said shakily. 'I didn't even *know* John when I met you.'

'Really?' He sounded unconvinced. 'I'm interested in what made you decide to leave so suddenly. Did the fact that I told you my uncle owned the flat and not me disappoint you? Couldn't you face the penury of being with a man who was just starting out?'

She opened her mouth to tell him. About Brooke. About the phone call; about meeting his aunt. Then let him wipe that supercilious expression off his face!

She was aware that she was glaring at him, her mouth opening to speak, her lips all moist with the new and rather vivid coral lipstick she'd applied for the journey, and she saw his gaze drawn to her mouth, saw his eyes narrow as if in hunger, but at that moment he frowned as the stewardess appeared with their lunch.

Saved by the bell, thought Elizabeth, slightly hysterically, not prepared to conduct the inevitable argument which would follow such a statement with delicious platters of food waiting to be unloaded on to their plates, by a stewardess who was panting like an eager puppy. Besides, she was aware that the atmosphere between them was strained enough—without her adding to it. And there were difficult times ahead. Far better prevarication than confrontation.

'Our son is sleeping,' she said quickly to the stewardess. 'Will——?'

'I can fix him something just as soon as he wakes,' said the stewardess soothingly, her eyes flashing with brief satisfaction over Elizabeth's ringless fingers before returning to rest sycophantically on Rick's face.

'Thanks,' he said briefly and, obviously expecting a more effusive response, she took the hint and left them.

Conventionally, Elizabeth had taken her own meal, but only picked at the food, however—Rick showed no such restraint, lancing giant prawns with his fork and following these with rare roast beef and salad. He glanced at her full plate.

'Not eating?'

'What does it look like?' she snapped.

Unexpectedly, he gave the merest hint of a smile. 'We shall continue our earlier conversation later, in private.' He dabbed at his mouth with a napkin. 'Did anyone ever tell you that your eyes flash like fireworks when you're angry?' he said unexpectedly.

How he could switch the charm on like a tap? she thought disgustedly. Well, you'll find I'm not as malleable as your Cheshire-cat stewardess! 'Frequently,' she answered back, in a bored voice. 'I usually point them in the direction of the nearest bookshop in search of a book entitled *Originality in Everyday Speech Patterns*. You should try reading it.'

'Oh, Elizabeth,' he said softly, gently shaking his head. 'You're a very stimulating woman to have an argument with.'

'Don't be so bloody patronising!'

His eyes sparked back, but then something alerted him and he moved slightly. 'Peter's stirring,' he murmured, then said in a slightly louder voice, 'Do eat your lunch, darling—dinner won't be for hours.'

'No, thank you, *darling*,' she mimicked. 'Something on this flight is making me feel extremely queasy.'

She saw him smile as he leaned over to talk to Peter who was slowly returning to the land of the living. 'Good sleep?'

'*Mmmmmm*!' Peter said, stretching his arms.

'Feel ready for some lunch?'

'You *bet*!'

'You're sounding good—a true American!' Rick laughed as he raised his hand a fraction, the movement bringing the stewardess to his side immediately.

He looked up at the uniformed specimen of feminine perfection. 'Let's try him with a cold roast beef sandwich,' he said. 'Heavy on the mayonnaise and hold the pickle.'

Suddenly, there was no Italian in him whatsoever, thought Elizabeth—he was the all-American boy—and he'd probably love to turn Peter into one as well. Over my dead body, she thought, as she leaned back in her seat and closed her eyes.

'Why don't we swap seats?' suggested Rick. 'Try to get some sleep, while I play cards with Peter.'

She complied and tried, but she could hear their quiet laughter, the calls of 'cheat', their enjoyment; while she felt as miserable as sin, not knowing what her reception was going to be like when they arrived at his home, or how she was going to co-exist under the same roof as him.

She could see the point of being pleasant while other people were around, but she could also see that, if being polite to one another meant his laying the charm on with a trowel, she'd prefer to going back to fighting again. Because it was amazing, and more than mildly disturbing, just how vulnerable she felt where he was concerned.

Although, financially, she had had no need of a career, intellectually at least she had wanted one. She felt that she owed it to herself after missing the opportunity to go to Oxford. She had flourished in her chosen career of accountancy, but it hadn't been easy in the early days of her training, with Peter just a baby. And then, later, after John's death, juggling with the demands of a demanding job and a young child—at times she had thought of jacking the whole thing in, but she hadn't and she had emerged, she thought, as a strong and independent woman in the process. And yet, at times, part of her got fed up with always having to 'cope'. Just this once it had been wonderful to allow Rick to take over, to let him organise their travel arrangements, leaving her

with only her packing to do. She had taken on the dual
role of mother and father to Peter for so long that it was
a relief to allow Rick to take on the father's role. And
Peter loved him doing it, that was for sure.

But though she had had many misgivings about this
trip and, much as though she wondered and sometimes
feared what the future would bring them, for Peter's
sake if nothing else, she was glad that they were here.
She *wanted* him to have the family she had always been
denied. And even though his immediate family would
consist of a stepsister whose very existence would serve
as a constant reminder of his father's duplicity—even
so, she had no right to deny Peter access to her.

Because undoubtedly he was much happier with the
new situation. The mock-family, she thought. Mummy,
Daddy and Peter. With them all going on holiday
together, and Mummy and Daddy not fighting. He had
accepted it with ease. As though, through meeting Rick,
a part of himself had been explained, like finding the
missing piece of a puzzle. And she, of all people, could
understand that. For there had been many times in her
life when she had yearned to know something of her
own family history. Some scrap of information on what
her father did, what her mother looked like. And, more
importantly, why they had abandoned her...

She sipped her champagne and turned her head to look
out of the window at the gold-dusted clouds which
looked so solid that she wouldn't have been surprised to
see a fat cherub perched on one of them.

She was surprised how easy it had been to shove all
her doubts and reservations about the prudence of this
trip aside. And you know why, an inner voice mocked.

Because it's infinitely the better of two evils. You convinced yourself that you wanted him out of your life,
but if he had simply gone you'd have been heartbroken.
And so would Peter.

She pushed her hand back through her hair, which
was now past her collar. She'd had neither the time nor
the inclination to get it cut these last few weeks. She had
forgotten how much softer and more feminine longer
hair could make you look and she wasn't sure she liked
that, either. She didn't want to feel soft and feminine,
she wanted to feel strong, and in control.

The rest of the journey passed in a daze of deferential
officials, of being taken quickly and smoothly into a
waiting limousine at Kennedy—a vehicle large enough
and luxurious enough to stun even Peter into silence—
and then of driving towards Newhaven.

Elizabeth gave a little cry as she took in the stunning
countryside when they left New York and moved deeper
into Connecticut.

Rick turned to her. 'What is it?'

Nothing could spoil the sudden rush of pleasure she
felt—a real 'holiday' feeling. 'Just that it's so *green*—
so fresh-looking!'

He smiled, as if her remark had given him pleasure.
'Somebody once said that Connecticut looks as if the
maid has just been in to clean, and I tend to agree with
them. You'll like Westport.'

That was what she was also afraid of: that she would
grow to like his lifestyle—his life—too much.

The journey to Rick's house was shorter than she had
imagined. Elizabeth didn't know what she had expected
to find when she arrived there; since she had been

working for him she had known that he was wealthy, but what she hadn't expected was wealth on this scale.

From the look of it, Westport, Connecticut was an expensive area at the best of times, but 'my house', as Rick described it when they drove in through wrought-iron gates, quite took her breath away. White, stately and magnificent, it stood in extensive grounds like a dazzling jewel, and at the back of the building she could see green lawns sloping down to the golden-white sand of what was obviously a private beach.

'You didn't tell me you had your own beach!' she accused.

'Didn't I?' he murmured softly.

'*Wow*!' exclaimed Peter. '*Wow*!'

'Like it?' he asked gently.

'*Do* I?'

Rick motioned for the chauffeur to stop the car. 'Let's walk,' he said.

The three of them got out of the limo, and walked up the driveway. In the distance, beyond some elegant fir trees, was the tantalising glimpse of glittering turquoise.

'Wow!' said Peter, for the third time. And he ran off towards the house.

'Peter!' called Elizabeth, half-heartedly, but Rick shook his head.

'Leave him,' he said. 'He'll come to no harm.'

Elizabeth turned to Rick. 'Do you own *all* this?'

There was a momentary pause. 'I do.'

'I see.' She mulled it over. 'You're a very powerful man, Rick,' she said eventually. 'Far more powerful than I imagined.'

There was a predatory glitter in his eyes. 'So I am,' he said, without boast. 'I made myself a promise many years ago that I would become a rich man.' His mouth tightened. 'Why? Does it turn you on?' he quizzed harshly.

Standing next to him, on that beautiful windswept landscape, she felt a crazy temptation to tell him that yes, he turned her on—oh, not his money or his possessions or his power. He had turned her on at eighteen, and he turned her on now. Always had and probably, she acknowledged with a sinking certainty, always would. A need to tell him that he was the only man she had ever loved came over her with a force as strong as a tidal wave, but she stood firmly in its path as it buffeted her, and it took all her strength to resist it.

Because the last few weeks of their 'truce' had lulled her into a false sense of security. She had to remember that he was only being 'polite' to her because it suited him to do so. Because he wanted Peter here, and she was part of the deal.

She turned to watch him, his olive-skinned profile beautifully etched against the sky as he gazed at his son running towards the vast house, and a great gush of sadness overwhelmed her—at the mockery they made of a family unit. It could have all been so different, she thought. How might Peter have been with this man as a father in the full sense of the word?

She forced herself to banish the thought. Because dwelling on what might have been would serve no purpose other than to make her sad, threaten the armour of her control; and here, in his house, she needed every ounce of control she had ever possessed. 'It's absolutely beautiful,' she said conventionally, staring at the house, when something *else* occurred to her. What if he had a live-in girlfriend over here? She hadn't thought to ask and yet it was highly likely that he had. Bitter experience had proved that he was a highly sexed man, untroubled by the strictures of fidelity.

'Who lives here?' she asked suddenly. 'With you?'

He turned, the eyes reflecting the glory of the sky, making them look more blue than green.

'The main house is mine,' he stated. 'And Jessie's.'

'There's just the two of you?'

'What were you expecting? A harem?' He shook his head. 'No, on second thoughts, don't answer that. I have a housekeeper—Claudia. She takes care of Jessie when I'm away on business, which, fortunately isn't too often. Her husband is my gardener. The building over there to the right is theirs. I prefer to have the house to myself. My mother and father live a few miles away—but they are regular visitors here to see Jessie.'

'I'm surprised you haven't built them a house here— there's certainly room enough for ten houses.'

He nodded. 'For sure. And my mother would no doubt be delighted with the arrangement—but I am an independent man, Elizabeth.' His eyes flashed. 'This is my world here. Mine alone.'

Mine alone. It sounded ominously like a warning. Don't get too entrenched, Elizabeth, that was what he was saying.

But knowing that did nothing to dampen her thoughts, because for a moment, standing against the skyline, he looked so dominant, so powerful, and so damned gorgeous that she was filled with an unbearable sense of longing—as potent as poison. At that moment, warning or no, she wanted him very much...

She forced herself to meet his piercing but unsmiling gaze, her own expression carefully schooled into the mild interest of a house-guest. 'Peter has reached the house,' she said. 'He's waiting for us.'

He nodded, putting his arm at the crook of her elbow, and even that impersonal touch made her senses sing. 'Let's go,' he said.

She walked by his side towards their child, her breath catching in her throat as she saw the front door of the house open, and a small, red-haired girl approach Peter. Scarcely realising that Rick's hand had tightened its grip on her elbow, they both stilled momentarily before renewing their pace towards the two children.

'Does Jessie know?' she asked quietly. 'That Peter is also your child?'

He paused, then nodded. 'Yes. I decided that it was better for her to know him on those terms from the very beginning.'

'What did you tell her?'

'Something on the lines of what you told Peter. That I lost contact with Peter long ago, and how glad I am to have found him.'

'Did she—mind?'

He looked at her quickly. 'She hasn't said very much about it. She can be capricious, I guess. She had an——' he hesitated '—unsettled babyhood. I suspect that learning to share a parent with a sibling is never easy—especially in such a way as this. What I hope I *have* done is to convince her that there is room in my heart for more than one child. That getting to know and learning to love Peter has absolutely no effect on the love I feel for her.'

She nodded, her head bent, not wanting him to see that the mere mention of love was enough to threaten to make her eyes unnaturally bright. God, she was a fool. The biggest fool in the world.

They were now within earshot. With Rick at her side, Elizabeth walked towards the two children, watching their tentative interaction.

Jessie looked up as she approached, her blue eyes wide and curious, and what struck Elizabeth with astonishment was how unlike Peter she was. She could see nothing of Rick in her, not initially, anyway.

She was slightly built, with hair the gentle ginger of autumn leaves, and a sweet little rosebud mouth which was trying to smile.

Elizabeth frowned in concentration as she watched the child turn towards her father. For one second, just one, she looked terribly familiar...

CHAPTER NINE

'DADDY! Daddy!' Jessie squealed excitedly, and threw herself into his arms, to be swung round in a tight bear-hug.

'Hello, honey,' he said gently. 'How's my girl?'

'She's fine,' Jessie smiled back, and stared at Elizabeth once more.

'Going to say hello to our guests?'

'I've already said hello to Peter. He's eight and he can't ride, but he can swim. Hello,' and wide blue eyes were turned up at Elizabeth, who couldn't nevertheless miss the little lines which creased her brow.

She's nervous, thought Elizabeth instantly. Just as nervous as I am, and her own smile widened in response.

'Hello,' she said shyly.

'Jessie, this is Elizabeth,' Rick said, in his deep voice.

'Hello, Jessie,' said Elizabeth softly and momentarily held both her hands out in greeting before letting them drop, not really surprised that Jessie's eyes should narrow with suspicion. 'We bought you a Sindy doll from England, with some clothes for her,' she said quickly, and then hoped that it didn't sound as if she was trying to buy favour. 'Do you like Sindy dolls?'

Jessie shrugged. 'They're OK. I have over a dozen already,' she answered, in a soft drawl, so like her father's.

Of course she did. 'But this is an *English* Sindy,' said Elizabeth, trying for a smile, glad that Rick was watchfully letting her deal with it, that he hadn't leapt in to reprimand his daughter, which would doubtless infuriate her even more.

'Is there a difference?'

Elizabeth smiled. 'Of course there is! She comes complete with her very own brolly and macintosh!'

'Brolly?' repeated Jessie.

'Umbrella,' translated Elizabeth.

'And macintosh?'

'That's a raincoat,' supplied her father drily.

'My favourite Sindy,' supplied Jessie, 'has a pink and gold ballgown!'

'Yuk!' said Peter expressively. 'Just like a girl!'

Jessie glared, obviously seeing this as a challenge. 'I like Action Man too, though,' she said haughtily.

'You *do*?' said Peter doubtfully.

'Love them.' There was a short pause. 'And I collect insects. Want to see?'

Peter's face indicated that he was hugely impressed by this piece of information. 'Can I, Mum?'

Elizabeth laughed, suddenly relieved. 'Of course you can. But it's an early night for you tonight; you're worn out with all the travelling.'

'Mum!'

'Peter—I *mean* it.'

Rick smiled. 'Your Mom's right. Dinner's early for you tonight, at seven. Jessie will show you your room, won't you, honey? It's right next to the insect house! Where's Claudia?'

Jessie grinned widely—Claudia was obviously a firm favourite—and the smile transformed her. Perfect white teeth and sparkling blue eyes. 'She's inside, cooking. Come on, Peter.'

The two children disappeared through the front door, and seconds later a small, dark woman who must have been in her sixties, with greying hair still streaked with darkness, smilingly opened the front door.

'Signor Rick, welcome home!' she beamed.

'Hello, Claudia.' He grinned affectionately, and it knocked about ten years off his face, thought Elizabeth with a little leap of her heart. 'Elizabeth—I'd like you to meet Claudia—my housekeeper. Claudia—this is Mrs Carson. She and her son will be staying with us for the summer. He's gone upstairs with Jessie.'

'I know. They rushed past me like the jet planes! I'm very pleased to meet you, Signora Carson.' She shook hands with Elizabeth and gave a slightly formal nod, and Elizabeth was aware of a brief but intense scrutiny from the small Italian woman.

'Come inside, Elizabeth, and I'll show you to your room. Can we have dinner at eight, please, Claudia?' And with his arm he indicated that Elizabeth should precede him.

She gave a little shiver, not at all sure that she wanted him showing her to her room, but she could hardly make a valid and polite objection in front of his housekeeper. So to focus her mind away from thoughts of beds, which had invaded her mind with a shocking clarity, Elizabeth made herself observe every inch of her surroundings as she followed him up the stairs. The vast entrance hall was like something out of a film set—a polished wooden floor from which a great staircase swept upwards and then opened out on either side. From the ceiling hung the most enormous chandelier that Elizabeth had ever seen. It reminded her of when she'd taken Peter to see *Phantom of the Opera*.

'This house is absolutely enormous,' she said for the second time, as they climbed the stairs.

He shot her a look. 'Nervous, Elizabeth?' he queried softly.

'Nervous? Why should I be?'

He gave a half-smile. 'You've gone as pale as a ghost. Is it the thought of bedrooms?'

It was so accurate that she felt as if he'd invaded her mind now, able to read her beleaguered thoughts. Her mouth and throat felt suddenly dry, breathing a task which required a gargantuan effort. Damn him, she thought stubbornly. And damn the effect he had on her.

'I'd like to look in on Peter before I do anything else,' she insisted.

'Of course,' he replied equably.

But even Peter could not save her from her own reactions, because when she and Rick peeped into the large 'den' it was to see two small heads bent companionably over a collection of small plastic dinosaurs.

'Do you need anything, Peter?' asked Elizabeth.

He scarcely looked up. 'I'm fine, thanks, Mum,' he said absently.

'You see?' said Rick. 'Everyone is happy.'

She said nothing as she followed him along to where he paused by a door.

'Here we are, Elizabeth—this is your room—just up the corridor from Peter.'

'Quite a long way up the corridor, it seems,' she challenged tartly.

He gave a low laugh as he pulled the door open, and she stepped over the threshold, something in his stance making her blood thunder like Niagara Falls, so that she hardly noticed the sumptuous furnishings of her room.

'It looks very comfortable,' she said quickly. 'Why are you shutting the door?'

'Because I want a little time alone with you.'

Her heart missed a beat. She pretended to look with interest around the room then turned back to face him, pushing her glasses further up her nose. 'I'm very tired, Rick. Can't this wait?'

He shook his head. 'No, it can't.'

'What do you want?' she asked impatiently.

He came closer, so that she could see the dark stubble which had begun to graze the strong line of his jaw, and she had to fight an urge to close her eyes and just let him take her in his arms.

Because there was no doubt at all that that was his intention; it was written all over his face—in the narrowed eyes which had darkened into ebony, and in the insistent pulse which she could see throbbing at the base of his throat. It was evident in every tightly coiled muscle which somehow managed to make its presence known through his clothing.

His arms encircled her waist. 'I want you, Beth,' he said huskily. 'I've never stopped wanting you, do you know that?'

She tried to pull away, but he wouldn't let her. 'Is that why you brought me to your house?' she whispered. 'So that you could make love to me?'

'A rather tortuous way of doing it, surely? To cross the Atlantic? It would have been much easier to make love to you in England. Although, in England, of course, we had the difficulty of your lover being around...' His words tailed off as his eyes travelled from her face to neck, to the silky mint-green shirt which covered her breasts.

'My *lover*?' she asked incredulously.

'Yes, your lover,' he ground out. 'Paul Meredith— your boss.'

'Paul is *not* my lover!'

'But he'd like to be, wouldn't he?' he whispered silkily.

'What business is that of yours?' she retaliated.

His eyes darkened. 'No matter. Here, my beautiful Elizabeth, we are alone—with none of the problems imposed by other interested parties...'

She wanted to answer him back in the same cynical smart-Alec manner but she couldn't do it, his very proximity was making her feel weak. She had vowed after that last episode that she was not going to respond to him, but her vow was becoming as distant as a memory from childhood. It was happening all over again, that slow, insistent fire that lit her from within. Surely this was as inevitable as breathing, this clamouring of her senses for him?

He had haunted her dreams and her waking moments, but, like the master of the situation he was, he had bided his time, so that now, when the inevitable approach was made, she had thought about it too long, dwelled on it too much, it had made her body hungry for him, and that made resistance not only difficult, but damn near impossible.

He shook his head as he gazed down at her, his eyes burning as they took in her flushed cheeks. He pulled her into his body so that she could feel how shockingly aroused he felt, and her body knew a feverish yearning to have him deep inside her.

Oh, God, how she wanted him. How good he made her feel, as though her body had never been alive except in his arms. So good... She stayed there in his arms, unmoving. Surely a minute more of this heaven wouldn't hurt?

'Rick,' she whispered pleadingly.

'What?' His mouth was against her mouth. How long now since he had touched her? How many weeks? Not since that night at her house when he'd nearly taken her on the floor of her sitting room. And she had fooled herself into thinking she was glad about it. She had mistakenly thought that it was a relief not to be touched by him, because his touch had the power to make all reason desert her.

And, sweet mercy, it was deserting her by the second. His hand massaged the small of her back, producing a sensual and languorous melting of her limbs, while the heat at the pit of her stomach had begun to build in a slow, insistent and tantalising blaze.

'Riccardo——' It was meant to be a protest, but her arms had somehow entwined themselves around his neck, and she felt his warm breath at her ear.

'What is it?' His voice was thick with desire.

'Please. Don't.'

'Please? Or don't?' he mocked.

'Don't.'

'Don't what?' She heard the smile as he spoke. 'I'm not doing anything, am I?'

Yet.

She looked up startled, unsure of whether someone had actually said it. 'Rick——' she began, but he shook his head.

'No. We've waited too long for this. You want this, Elizabeth—you want it as much as I do. Tell me, honestly, that you want me to stop, and I'll stop.'

She opened her mouth to speak but no words came; instead his lips touched against hers so lightly that she started trembling as violently as if someone had given her a profound shock.

He drew back then, and looked at her, mild surprise clouding the amazing eyes as he observed her reaction. 'It's all right,' he murmured. 'It's all right,' and, with his arms still locked tightly around her, he moved towards the bed, and drew her down beside him, so that she lay on the counterpane, her head on a soft downy pillow, with Rick propped up on an elbow, staring down at her curiously.

Her face and her body felt rosy-warm, suffused with the unquenchable flames of the most delicious fire. It was simply too easy to succumb to the temptation, and she shook her head from side to side, like someone trying to rid themselves of an insect. 'It's not all right,' she said, but her voice sounded already slumberous, her misgivings already forgotten as her body greedily anticipated his touch.

He gave a slow, slow smile as he carefully lifted her glasses off and placed them on the bedside table. 'Then let me make it all right. Shall I do that, Elizabeth?'

She closed her eyes just for a second, so that she couldn't see what he was doing, as if observation would make her an accomplice, feeling instead his fingers skating down over her silky shirt to the valley between her breasts. She heard him draw in a breath, and her own breathing shuddered as one finger moved inside the moist V, and as he did so she could feel the tips of each breast grow deliciously and uncomfortably hard, and she knew that they must be outlined against her shirt as if cast in iron. And when, because she could no longer resist doing so, she opened her eyes once more, it was to delight in the rapt preoccupation on his face as he began to touch her.

'You, my beautiful Elizabeth, are a creature of such delectable contrasts,' he whispered as he began to unbutton her blouse, and to her everlasting shame she let him. 'On the outside there is that prim, efficient exterior—the crisp suits which hide how much of a woman you are beneath. But underneath—ah!' he sighed. 'Long, long legs in silk stockings—they betray you as much as the high heels you wear. And now this.' He had unbuttoned all the way down to the waistband of her skirt, and the shirt fell open to reveal her lush, creamy breasts—straining furiously against the insubstantial wisp of cream lace and satin which confined them. He had the front clasp of her bra unclipped in an instant, and her breasts were at long last freed. She felt deliciously wanton as they were laid bare. Long, sensual fingers began to tiptoe with tantalising skill over the heavy mounds and she gave a little cry.

'You see,' he smiled. 'See how much you want me? I wonder,' his voice husked, 'if you want me quite as much as I want you?'

He sucked in another breath, and she stared up into his face, shocked by the look of almost primitive desire she surprised—the eyes just glittering slits, their light colour completely obliterated by the dilated jet of the pupil. Every fine feature in his face was clearly discernible, the olive skin stretched back tightly over muscle and bone. Even his mouth, that full and sensual mouth with its occasionally quirky curves at the corner—now, it was unrecognisable as his mouth, it was a hard, unquivering line, held still only through what Elizabeth could see was rigid control.

He saw the look in her eyes and he nodded, shifting his position slightly, as though to ease the tension. 'Yes,' he said. 'You see what you can do to me. Now feel.' And he took her hand, ran it down over the hard-packed muscle of his chest which lay beneath the fine shirt, and guided it between his thighs to rest it there, and she felt his fierce hardness throbbing beneath her fingers, before sanity prevailed, and she snatched her hand away, as if scalded.

For this was not the man who had made love to her through night and day during that mad weekend of their youth. He was years older, years more experienced, and with those years had come a mature desire which thrilled her with terror. In his hands she was as pliable as warm dough. She had to put a stop to this—now!

She made a small sound at the back of her throat, and as he laughed, his hand moved to brush with deliberate provocation over her breast.

'I know. It's inconvenient, isn't it, Elizabeth, to feel this way?' He moved his mouth to whisper against her ear. 'I have to have you, do you know that?'

Her wordless protest died the instant she felt his other hand move sensuously up her leg, his hand finding the bare skin between stocking-top and panties, and as his fingers crept slowly upwards she felt the heat threaten to engulf her completely.

He gave a low, anguished moan as he reached the top of her thigh, and his fingers began to stroke enticing circles of magic.

Perhaps if he had remained silent then their love-making would have gone on to its inevitable conclusion. But he didn't, and his bitter words invaded her euphoria like gatecrashers at a wedding.

'Did your husband touch you this way? Did he? Did *he* make you feel this way?' he taunted her, as he splayed his hand possessively over the moist silk of her panties, and the spell was broken in an instant.

Wriggling from underneath him, she jumped off the bed and stood up, her eyes flicking dismissively over him, her colour heightening in intensity as she observed the very obvious signs of just how aroused he was.

'One of these days your libido is going to get you into even more trouble,' she declared hotly, her voice trembling almost as much as her body.

He rolled over on to his back, his hands propped behind his head, his gaze as steady as a rock, though his breathing was not. 'I could say the same for you.'

She shook her head. 'Not really, Rick. I'm one of those curiously old-fashioned people who don't believe in having more than one person on the go at a time.'

His eyes narrowed. 'If you're trying to make a point, Elizabeth, then go right ahead, but spare me the riddles.'

At that moment she really and truly hated him. For his deceit and his lies. For daring to criticise *her*, when so much of his own behaviour had been underhand. But she hated herself even more, for being unable to shake off the desire she felt for him, which had just manifested itself in another shameful near-capitulation on the bed.

'Do you really want to know why I ran out that morning all those years ago? For a supposedly intelligent man, I'm surprised that the real reason has never occurred to you?' She paused as she saw his look of attention, savouring her small moment of triumph. 'It was because I discovered that our brief little fling wasn't all the wine and roses it seemed. I found out, you see. I knew that you had a fiancée, Rick—I knew about Brooke!'

Not a flicker of shock or guilt crossed his face, the cool, steady gaze remained, only the merest elevation of a seemingly casual eyebrow an indication that he was interested in hearing what she had to say.

'I woke up in the middle of the night to find that you weren't beside me—you were on the balcony,' she declared hotly. 'Standing there, wrapped in a towel. I heard you cursing—over and over again—and it seemed fairly obvious to me that you were regretting what had happened. Then you went into the bathroom, and while you were in the shower—the telephone rang and your fiancée mistook me for the maid! Your *fiancée*,' she emphasised, the words she had bottled up for so long coming out in one poisonous rush.

Their eyes met.

'I suppose you have a good reason for keeping this remarkable piece of information to yourself all these weeks?' he answered coolly.

She stared at him, astounded. He was doing, she realised, what all good barristers did. They attacked, went on the offensive, just as he was doing now. She returned his cool look with one of her own. 'You know what they say,' she said softly. 'About the most effective weapons being the ones we conceal.'

'And you need weapons against me, do you, Elizabeth?'

She shrugged. 'I wasn't taking any chances. At the time I feared that you might try and take Peter away from me.'

He looked at her curiously. 'But not any more?'

She didn't even hesitate. 'No,' she admitted honestly. 'I don't believe you would. I think you love Peter enough not to try to spoil his happiness.'

His mouth twisted. 'One must be grateful for small mercies, I suppose.'

He had also used another well-known courtroom ploy, thought Elizabeth; he had managed to steer the conversation away from its original, uncomfortable subject. 'What I mentioned just now, about Brooke. Can you deny it?' she asked quietly.

A moment's silence.

'No,' he said shortly, and, leaning his head back against the pillow, he shut his eyes almost wearily, his face drained of colour.

'*Dad-dy*!'

A small girl's voice came from behind the closed door, and he swung his legs over the bed immediately, standing

up and tucking his shirt back into the waistband of his
trousers, his eyes suddenly and coldly forbidding.

'Stay here,' he ground out. 'And for God's sake button
your blouse up. I'll deal with it.'

She stood completely immobile for a moment,
watching as he walked over to the door and began to
turn the key and she realised to her horror that he *had*
locked it—and she hadn't even noticed! He shut it quietly
behind him. In control, she thought bitterly. As always.

She closed her eyes in despair as she fumbled to do
her bra back up with hands that were shaking, staring
at the bed, at the rumpled counterpane with distaste,
wondering just how far they would have gone if he had
not cheapened their lovemaking by asking her about
John.

She sat down at her dressing-table, staring at her reflection as she buttoned her blouse back up with trembling fingers. She must get herself together.

She was here for seven weeks, that was all—to give
Peter the chance to get to know his father and his father's
family. And her only role was as Peter's mother. She
was there because *he* was there, that was all.

She was an adult now, not a teenager, and she must
acknowledge that there was still, undoubtedly, an in-
tensely strong physical attraction between them which
seemed to have little to do with liking—in fact, Rick
seemed to dislike her just as much as she disliked him.

She had no doubt that his bed was hers for the duration of her stay if she cared to take him up on it. But,
quite apart from what had happened between them in
the past, she knew now that she was not a casual
person—she doubted that she could ever willingly enter

into a love-affair knowing that it was for a limited duration only. No matter how much her body craved such a union. And that would be all that Rick would ever offer her.

She gazed at her reflection. Without her glasses she appeared so much younger—with cheeks flushed pink, her hair beginning to fall into waves around the nape of her long neck. She rose to her feet shakily, went and picked up her glasses from the bedside table and put them back on.

It was time she started exercising a little self-control. She *must* try and swamp the physical attraction she felt for Rick. The situation was difficult enough without her compounding it by leaping straight into his bed, however much she wanted to.

There was a rap on the door. She reached for her handbag and sat down at the dressing-table to rake a comb through her hair, smoothing the ruffled locks into some kind of style. 'Come in.'

She turned in her chair as a whirlwind of movement indicated that her son had arrived, an excited-looking Jessie on his heels, and, behind them both, Rick, his stare steady as it sought her out over the two small heads. There was no hint as to what he might be feeling, and not one trace of aborted passion could she detect in *his* face.

But then she looked at Peter, who was bubbling over with happiness. This must be a whole wonderful new world for him, she thought with sadness.

'How's it going, darling?' she asked softly, then turned to Jessie. 'Did you play with the dinosaurs?'

'We're missing a heterodontosaurus,' frowned Peter.

We're. Already he was part of the family, while she must remain the outsider. Elizabeth swallowed but managed a smile. 'You don't say?' she teased. 'And life isn't worth living, of course—without a heterodontosaurus?'

Rick smiled too, but his smile came more naturally. It *would* do, thought Elizabeth; he isn't the one who stands to lose anything.

'Tomorrow we can go and look for a——?'

He looked at both children quizzically.

'*Heterodontosaurus*!' they chorused triumphantly.

'I'll take your word for it,' he said gravely. He looked over at Elizabeth and raised his eyebrows slightly when he saw her face. 'Tell you what, Jessie,' he suggested. 'Why don't you take Peter down to Claudia—see if you can persuade her to give you something to drink?'

With a pounding of feet, they obeyed him, and Elizabeth rose to her feet to face him, but his superior height gave him a psychological advantage.

'Rick——' she began.

'Let me guess,' he interrupted, giving her a long, considering stare, his thumb and forefinger rubbing at the dark stubble of his chin. 'You're about to give me a lecture about my lustful designs on your lovely body?'

She gave him a look which by rights should have turned him to stone. 'Right first time, and I'd rather it didn't happen again,' she said, forcing her voice to be neutral. 'Co-existing will be much less traumatic if we keep things purely platonic.'

He gave her a long, hard look. 'You could always try saying "no",' he mocked.

Elizabeth's mouth fell open. 'You bastard!' she said softly, but there wasn't a trace of reaction to the insult on his harsh and implacable features.

He carried on as if she hadn't spoken, his voice suddenly intense. 'But you can't say no, can you, Elizabeth? Because what happens when I touch you is far more powerful than your wish to keep me at bay. And you can't stop yourself from wanting me, can you?'

She carefully schooled her own features into a replica of his impassiveness, but it was no good—his cool and watchful expression set her fingers itching with irritation, and she was half tempted to pick the silver-backed hairbrush from the dressing-table and to send it spinning in his direction. Perhaps he saw the slight movement, for he gave an amused smile.

'Won't do you any good, Elizabeth. You see—like our friend the heterodontosaurus—my skull is able to withstand hard knocks.'

He opened the door. 'Anything you need, just call me.'

A return ticket back to England was about the only thing she could think of right then.

CHAPTER TEN

ELIZABETH should have slept the few hours left before dinner, but she didn't even bother trying. She was too strung up to sleep—and not just mentally, she acknowledged wryly. That little session of interrupted foreplay on the bed earlier had left her feeling completely strung-out. Little beads of sweat broke out on her brow as she remembered Rick slowly baring her breasts...

Sex, or rather the lack of it, had never been a problem for her. Not even after that wonderful initiation with Rick all those years ago. *Especially* not after that. The discovery that she had been betrayed and the traumatic aftermath of finding out that she was pregnant had been enough to make her vow never to let anyone get that close to her ever again.

She had married John both admiring and respecting him, had wanted to be a good wife to him in every sense of the word. But John had not wanted her physical commitment to him, for the disease which was slowly wrecking his body had killed all his own needs.

And, a couple of years after his death, she had even gone out on a few dates. But nothing. There had been no one to tempt her even remotely out of her self-imposed chastity—although most of her dates had tried. But it had been like dancing without the music. A kiss had just been an intrusion, where a kiss of Rick's had seemed like a melding together of two souls.

She shook her head a little as she towel-dried her hair.
The melding together of two souls indeed! How he would
laugh if he knew how her adolescent romanticism where
he was concerned had not diminished over the years.

Why couldn't she allow maturity and reason to dictate
that she felt nothing for him other than that they were
linked by the bond of their child?

You know why, came the unwelcome answer. Because
you loved him then, madly and passionately, and you've
never really stopped loving him, even after all that he's
done, all that's happened.

'No!' She spoke the word aloud in desperation. It
couldn't be so. She didn't want it to be so. She didn't
love him. Surely fate wouldn't be so cruel? Hadn't she
had enough to cope with, without being inextricably
linked emotionally to a man who desired her body, but
who had never even shown her the courtesy of fidelity?

It was far more likely that she was simply using love
as a justification for the fact that she desired him just
as much as he did her, because love could justify
anything.

But if that were the case, then why had she never forgotten him all these years, why had never a day passed
when she hadn't thought of him and secretly yearned
for him? Not just because of Peter, but because she'd
never got him out of her system.

And if her feelings for him were merely rooted in the
physical, then there was nothing stopping her from
sharing his bed while she was here—this was the nine-
ties, after all. As he had bluntly and arrogantly told her
earlier, there was some sizzling chemistry between them
which fired into life as soon as he touched her. She could,

she knew, have the affair of a lifetime with Rick. But that wouldn't be enough, she recognised. She would leave here after the summer break and she would go back to England with her heart in further tatters...

Because he *didn't* care—he was ruled by instincts far baser than love. And, if she gave herself to him, he would take everything she had to give—leaving her with nothing.

She opened up the wardrobe door and selected a dress, choosing a starkly cut navy linen dress with matching low-heeled court shoes which made her look crisp, efficient and, she hoped, a little forbidding. She kept make-up to a minimum, and her only decoration was a single strand of pearls which John had given to her on their wedding-day.

Earlier, she had checked on Peter to find that Rick was about to take the two of them swimming in the pool. Carefully averting her eyes from the sight of his tanned and muscular legs beneath the towelling gown he wore, she had crouched down anxiously to peer into her son's face, amazed that he should have settled in so well, and so quickly.

'You're not tired, darling? Wouldn't you rather have a nap than a swim?'

'*Mummy!*' She might have been offering him a choice between a plate of cold cabbage or a plate of ice-cream from the look on his face. 'I'm fine. I'm going to race Jessie.'

'Girls are fantastic, boys are elastic!' chanted Jessie.

'I'm inclined to agree with you,' said Elizabeth ruefully, still not meeting Rick's eyes.

And now, as she pushed Peter's room door open, she could see that he was already in bed in his pyjamas, and that Rick was just switching off the light in the adjoining bathroom.

She avoided that darkly enigmatic gaze and went and sat on the edge of the bed. 'Night night, darling,' she whispered. 'Have you eaten anything?'

'Uh-huh! After swimming we had some of Claudia's pasta—and Daddy showed me how to eat it like an Italian. You just twirl it round your fork, you know—you don't even have to use a spoon! It was fantabulous,' yawned Peter.

'That's good,' said Elizabeth, a trifle drily.

'*Then* Daddy gave me a bath!'

Elizabeth blinked. Somehow it was difficult to imagine the tycoon up to his elbows in suds!

'Did he? That was nice.'

'Mmm. Night night, Mummy,' said Peter sleepily.

'Night night darling.' Elizabeth lightly brushed Peter's forehead with a kiss and rose to her feet. Rick was waiting for her by the door.

He too had dressed for dinner—in charcoal-grey trousers with a snowy shirt and an extravagant silk tie in a startling shade of aquamarine, which matched his eyes exactly. The ebony of his hair had been combed into neat, dark waves, and she remembered how ruffled and flushed he had been on her bed, earlier. Her foolish heart thundered but she smiled at him as courteously as if he were nothing more than a client.

'Who is eating with us?' she asked quietly. 'Is it just the two of us?'

He nodded, a cool look of enquiry in his eyes. 'It is. Why, Elizabeth?' the deep voice mocked. 'Does that bother you?'

'Why should it?' she retorted. 'I'm hungry enough not to care about who I dine with!'

He gave a small laugh and made a gesture with his head towards the sleeping form in the bed.

'Let's go down,' he said softly. 'They're both exhausted. What with all the swimming and football, they've worn themselves out. And me,' he finished, with a wry elevation of his eyebrows, which didn't fool Elizabeth for a minute.

'I don't believe you,' she said. 'Nothing could tire you out. You know what they say—that the devil looks after his own.'

'Now, Elizabeth,' he reprimanded. 'Remember what we agreed? You mustn't use that sharp tongue of yours to berate me all evening.'

'I'd prefer to call it accurate, rather than sharp,' she returned spiritedly. 'And I'm agreeing to nothing.'

'As expected.' He gave a smile. 'Let's go down and eat.'

She allowed him to lead her down the magnificent staircase, past the vast, glittering chandelier, and he gave her a short tour of the ground floor of the house—all elegant, high-ceilinged rooms, each room furnished in a highly individual and dramatic style. The dining-room was painted a vivid yellow, with blue glosswork and small pieces of blue china—making it look as if they had been transported to the south of France.

Another room was ochre-hued, the furnishings and drapes in contrasting tartans!

It was unexpected and delightful enough for her to be able to put her troubled thoughts aside and to exclaim uninhibitedly, 'Who designed all this?' Then wished she hadn't—it would have bound to have been Brooke.

'I did, last year.'

'Not a professional decorator's touch in sight?'

'I *hate* professional decorators,' he said, with feeling.

'So do I,' she agreed unwillingly.

Eventually he led her into a small book-lined room, with two chintz-covered adjacent sofas, and a crystal bowl full of blowsy red roses standing on a polished table, scenting the room with their heady fragrance. It was like a warm haven, she thought. She found herself unobtrusively glancing around the room, and realised that she was searching for something. Photos of Brooke. But she looked in vain.

'Wine?' he enquired.

'Thank you.'

To Elizabeth's surprise dinner was not a trial, nor an endurance test. On the contrary, Rick was very good company indeed, but then he always had been, except that now, nine years later, he was even more assured and self-possessed, if that were possible. He was evidently on his best behaviour and she responded in kind.

She registered that she was in fact being manipulated by the sheer potency of his charm. Evidently a man who was disproportionately and quite unfairly rich, good-looking and personable did not normally have to try very hard, especially with women. But he *was* trying hard tonight, and it was as impossible not to be affected by that, as it was to ignore the beauty of her surroundings.

Perhaps the wine helped, and the quality of the excellent Italian cooking which was discreetly served up by Claudia. He might be simply playing the dutiful host in order not to embarrass her in front of his staff, she realised, but even that could not detract from the fact that he had a superb sense of humour. She found herself dropping her guard in spite of everything which had happened earlier. They ended up discussing the comparative complexities between an English and American legal system, and Elizabeth found it thoroughly absorbing to do battle with him mentally.

She was on her third cup of coffee when her eyes were drawn to his wrist, startled to see that it was past midnight. She drained the last of her coffee and pushed her cup away.

'I didn't realise it was so late.'

'No. Me neither.' He gave her a quite unnerving stare, the blue-green eyes even more glittering even than usual.

'I'd better go to bed,' she said, in a voice suddenly husky.

He nodded. 'As you say—it's late.'

'Goodnight.' She headed for the door, terrified that he might see how easily she could be seduced by a few kind words and some good conversation.

'Oh, Elizabeth——'

She hesitated, her hand on the handle of the door. 'Yes?'

'My parents are anxious to meet Peter. And you. I thought it all might be too new to you to inflict a dinner on you this evening, or even this week—but I'd like to invite them over early next week.'

She nodded. 'That's fine.' Then something jarred, the memory of the beautiful blonde woman, standing in the doorway of his uncle's flat, all those years ago in London. 'Just your parents?' she asked tentatively.

'Who else would there be?'

'I thought you had an uncle and an aunt you were close to.'

He frowned. 'So I have—but I don't see them too often.'

She let out a small breath. Thank God. She would rather that particular memory wouldn't have to be resurrected in front of someone else. But as long as she lived she would remember the look of pitying scorn on the woman's face, leaving Beth to shrink away like a dog going away to die.

He hesitated, as if he was about to say something more, then apparently changed his mind. 'Goodnight,' he said, and began to pour himself another cup of coffee.

CHAPTER ELEVEN

IN THE week which followed, Elizabeth found herself surprised on more than one occasion—dinner that first night had *not* been a fluke. They *could* exist companionably.

Consequently she found herself relaxing enough to genuinely enjoy the days, and there was no doubt in her mind whatsoever that Peter was having a great time.

Jessie was a different matter. Although she seemed to have accepted their presence there with a commendable lack of jealousy or resentment and would play quite happily with Peter for most of the time, at others she would retreat into silence, her little pixie face unsmiling, the big blue eyes unashamedly miserable. Was she still missing her mother? wondered Elizabeth, her heart going out to the small girl. Even after six years? Very probably.

Not that she ever mentioned her mother, and there were certainly no photographs or portraits of Brooke within the house—but Elizabeth could understand that, too. Sometimes memories were just too painful to live with.

What did surprise her was that Rick made no mention of Brooke either, not in front of her, anyway, but perhaps that was simply diplomacy. Maybe he'd even removed the photographs before she'd arrived—but then surely that would have hurt Jessie badly?

Or perhaps he too, missed her so much that he could
not bear to speak her name, or to look on her picture . . .

And if the circumstances had been any different, then
Elizabeth might have felt free to ask Rick about his wife.
But she couldn't. And somehow, not knowing, the very
absence of any reminders of the woman, made Brooke
loom large and threatening in Elizabeth's imagination.
The ever-present ghost in this strange and beautiful place.

The days continued to unfold.

They went sightseeing around New York. They swam
every day in Rick's pool or picnicked on the beach. Rick
drove them through the beautiful countryside, which was
predominantly densely wooded forests. He took them to
the State parks where Peter tried canoeing for the first
time, and where they hiked, and boated. Every evening
they ate early, the four of them, at seven. Elizabeth preferred this, and so did the children. And of course it
was much easier to remain unaffected by Rick if she was
able to keep herself busy by immersing herself in the
demands of childcare.

One evening, after supper, Rick suggested chess to
Peter.

'Can you play?' he asked.

'Oh, *yes*,' said Peter proudly. 'Mummy taught me.
She plays brilliantly.'

Elizabeth found herself staring into a pair of blue-
green eyes.

'I know she does.'

'How?'

'Because she used to beat me!'

'*Did* she?'

The eyes looked distinctly amused at her discomfiture. 'Sure she did.'

'Can you play, Jessie?' asked Elizabeth quickly.

Jessie was biting her bottom lip. 'No, I can't,' she said listlessly.

Rick frowned. 'I should have taught her myself.' Their eyes met. 'But I haven't played in years.'

The memories of those long-ago chess days really *were* too poignant to evoke. 'Lots of people don't like chess, of course, Jessie,' interjected Elizabeth hastily. 'And some people say—though I'm not one of them—that it's a thing which men do better than women—like map-reading. But if you like, I could try teaching you. See if you enjoy it.'

The big blue eyes positively glowed. 'Would you? Oh, yes, please.'

So, after supper, Elizabeth began to take Jessie into the study, where she could teach her quietly, and she started to look forward to the sessions, growing to like the small girl immensely, because, as she got to know Elizabeth better, Jessie grew less inclined to play the bored little rich girl. And it was gratifying for Elizabeth to hear the sound of her laughter ringing out as she attempted to master the rudiments of the complex game.

It evidently made Rick happy, too. One night when the children had gone to bed, and they'd been sitting reading—or rather, he had—for Elizabeth found it difficult to concentrate on the page of text when his long legs were sprawled with such careless elegance just a few yards away—he put his newspaper down and turned to her.

'You're very kind to Jessie—thank you.'

She shook her head. 'There's no need to thank me; the pleasure is mine—I enjoy teaching her.'

'I know. It isn't just the chess—you're especially thoughtful towards her. Tell me, are you always so good with children?'

'I don't actually have that much to do with them, apart from Peter.' She saw his look of bemusement and tried to explain. 'I just feel for Jessie, and for Peter—they've both lost a parent——' She saw his face, and corrected herself immediately. 'I know that in Peter's case he's found you now—but to some extent you're rudderless and insecure if you grow up with only one parent——'

'Or none?' he interrupted shrewdly.

She bit the inside of her lip. 'I'm not looking for sympathy——'

'But growing up without *either* parent...?'

'Isn't particularly recommended by child psychologists,' she said bluntly. 'And now, do you think we could finish our analysis session?'

'Did you never try to find them?' he asked curiously.

He was like a dog with a bone! She stared at him in exasperation. 'I only asked once. The house mother I had at the time was not known for her love of children— she took great pleasure in telling me that I'd been dumped—literally—in a cardboard box outside the police station.'

'Bitch,' he said, very quietly, and she found herself dazzled by the understanding that fired in the depths of those blue-green eyes.

'Do you mind if we don't talk about it any more?' she asked.

'Certainly.' He lifted the heavy silver pot. 'More coffee?'

'Thank you.' The large pot which was provided each evening was strong and aromatic. Elizabeth accepted one of the tiny silver-rimmed cups.

There was silence for a moment. He sipped his coffee and didn't pick the newspaper back up, just continued to regard her steadily from beneath the thick, dark lashes. 'You look very beautiful tonight,' he said softly.

'Thank you,' she replied, in an equally quiet voice, colour stealing into her cheeks at the compliment. Suddenly shy, she swapped her coffee for the small glass of Grappa he'd given her, wondering what had possessed her to bring the most frivolous garment in her entire wardrobe. And then to wear it.

They had spent a lazy day picnicking and playing beach games, and Elizabeth had felt flushed with warmth and sunshine, more relaxed than she could remember feeling in years.

After her shower she had been filled with a sudden and very feminine desire to dress up, to look her prettiest—and, now that she had, she wasn't at all sure that she should have done, not with Rick staring at her in that openly appreciative way.

But isn't that what you wanted? a voice mocked.

The dress was pink, with tiny shoestring straps over the fitted bodice, showing the golden-cream of her lightly tanned skin. In contrast to the close fit of the bodice, the skirt of the dress was short, filmy pleated chiffon— the diaphanous material hinting at the shadowed shape of her thighs.

Suddenly Elizabeth could stand no more, and she quickly stood up. 'It's late, she said. 'I'm going to bed now.'

He stood up, and her heart quickened. 'Me, too,' he said.

Elizabeth's mouth became as dry as dust. Most evenings he stayed up long after she'd retired to bed. One night she had woken suddenly, long after midnight, thinking she'd overheard a sound and had gone into check on Peter, finding, to her surprise as she peered over the banister, that light spilled on to the floor from underneath Rick's closed study door.

Her hands were trembling as they walked side by side up the side staircase and Elizabeth hid them in the knife-pleats of her filmy skirt.

And outside her door, as she had somehow known he would, he paused.

'You know, Elizabeth,' he said, in the deep, caressing voice, 'that you really mustn't wear such a gown again. Not——' and his hand reached out, his fingers going to the tip of her chin, to rest there with butterfly-soft seduction '—not,' he continued, 'unless you want me to kiss you.'

She stared up at him with wide, bright eyes, realising with a sudden sadness that this was how it *might* have been. The slow, civilised courtship—the companionship which grew out of shared times. Not the wildly impetuous physical spark which had marred their relationship from the word go.

'No,' she said quietly, afraid that she might start to cry. 'I don't want you to kiss me,' she lied, then, with a return of spirit added, 'Don't worry, your comments have been noted. I'll wear something eminently suitable tomorrow evening.'

'I don't think that such a garment exists,' he said drily, and walked off towards his own room. 'Goodnight, Elizabeth.'

'Goodnight,' she echoed as she opened her door, thinking that she really wouldn't have minded if he'd ridden roughshod over her wishes and kissed her anyway, then lay awake imagining what might have happened if he had—which made for a very restless and frustrated night indeed.

Jessie learnt chess quickly, and the four of them started playing most evenings after supper, Elizabeth listening to the occasional sound of Rick's deep laugh, thinking that this must be what paradise must be like, but a paradise of limited duration. A precarious paradise...

Peter had settled in so well, and so quickly, that she absolutely dreaded the thought of taking him away, and back to the prospect of a cold and rainy winter in England.

Elizabeth was jumpy all during the day of his parents' visit for dinner, changing her dress at least three times in an effort to look somehow 'respectable'.

'You're nervous,' observed Rick, when she finally came downstairs, dressed in the severely cut navy dress she'd worn on the first night.

'Well, what do you think?' she demanded, taking the glass of wine he offered her and sipping it gratefully. 'I don't even know what you've told them about me.'

'Everything.'

'And what's everything?'

'They know that we met, and parted. They know that I discovered we have a son.'

'And what did they say? I suppose they must think I'm some kind of——'

He interrupted her. 'They are not unreasonable people, Elizabeth. And they certainly wouldn't presume to make a snap judgement, especially not without having met you.' There was the distant peal of a doorbell. 'That sounds like them.'

He went to answer the door and Elizabeth rose to her feet slowly, his words doing little to reassure her as he ushered the older couple through the door. She expected to see all kinds of negative emotions written on the face of the elegantly clothed woman who walked towards her, but to her surprise, she saw nothing other than polite smiles as Rick's parents walked towards her.

His father was, she knew, American. A tall, striking man in his late sixties with the same strong features which Rick had inherited, along with those light blue-green eyes. He smiled at her and shook her hands with a grip so firm it threatened to crush her fingers. Bizarrely, she remembered a house mother at the orphanage telling her to always trust a man with a firm handshake. And Rick had the same...

From his Italian mother Rick had inherited his smooth olive skin and the ebony hair and brows and lashes. With a start, Elizabeth realised that there was something of Peter in his paternal grandmother, and something stirred to life within her—the realisation that it was possible for Peter to have what she had missed out on all her life— the opportunity to learn more about himself through his extended family.

'Elizabeth,' Mrs Masterton held a beautifully manicured hand out, and the easy use of her Christian name disarmed Elizabeth immediately.

'I'm pleased to meet you, Mrs Masterton,' she said, smiling.

'No, no—you must call me Enza—I insist!' the older woman smiled back. 'Riccardo——' she pronounced it with an attractive, lilting accent '—has told me a great deal about you.'

'Oh?' Elizabeth couldn't for the life of her imagine what he'd had to say.

'How well you've done—to qualify as an accountant at the same time as bringing—Peter up. We're very much looking forward to meeting him.' Her eyes searched Elizabeth's face, and Elizabeth could sense that her complexion was entirely drained of blood. 'Come and sit down, my dear,' she said softly. 'You've had a long and traumatic day, waiting for us to arrive!' Her dark eyes flashed understandingly. 'But I think you will find we don't bite!'

Mr Masterton senior nodded. 'Only Claudia's delicious pasta, anyway! Now before we go any further— what does a man have to do to get a drink around here?'

They all laughed, Elizabeth, too, suddenly feeling as though a weight *had* been lifted, and they sat drinking champagne before going through into dinner, Elizabeth's appetite miraculously recovered as she ploughed her way through the delicious meal.

'Claudia has been marvellous,' confided Enza. 'She helped look after Jessie when she was a baby, when her mother——'

'Mother——' Rick's voice interrupted warningly. 'Your soup's getting cold.'

The atmosphere at the table had become electric. Elizabeth put a piece of bread in her mouth simply for something to do, before Rick's father came to the rescue.

'I believe I've had some dealings with your boss— Paul Meredith, isn't it?'

Elizabeth nodded, glad enough to lose herself in the subject of stocks and shares and the question of the European Community with Rick's father, wondering what Enza had been about to say about Brooke. It doesn't *matter*, she thought fiercely. It's none of your business.

They took their leave just before midnight, arranging to visit for the whole of the following day, in order to start to get to know Peter.

It was only when Rick was seeing them off in the hallway that she realised that her social graces left something to be desired, since she had been curled up on the sofa all evening in her stockinged feet! She went back into the dining-room to find the shoes she'd kicked off beneath the table, and stooped down to slide them on to find Rick standing staring down at her, a thoughtful expression in his eyes.

'Relaxed enough to kick your shoes off? I think we can take it that the evening was a success, then?'

'You know it was.'

'Better than I could ever have anticipated.' He snuffed out a candle between his thumb and forefinger, and the sudden loss of light sent mysterious shadows into the hollows of his face. 'You don't need me to tell you how much they liked you.'

'The feeling was mutual,' she said evenly. 'Why do I feel as though I've just passed some sort of test?'

There was a moment's silence. 'I had forgotten,' he said, in an indefinable tone she'd never heard him use before, 'that you were always the most intelligent woman I'd met in my life, but I'd never put astuteness down as one of your qualities.'

'It's too late for semantics,' she said tiredly. 'This day has been quite long enough. I liked your parents too. And now I'm going to bed.'

She knew that he stood there, just watching her, as she wearily made her way up the magnificent curve of the staircase.

CHAPTER TWELVE

ELIZABETH fanned herself with a hat as she walked towards the pool, knowing that she could no longer put off the inevitable. How could six weeks have slipped by without her noticing? It had been with complete shock that she had registered the date on the newspaper this morning—they were nearly into September and it was time to think about going home.

Surprisingly, it had turned out to be one of the most contented periods of her life, and she didn't want to think about it coming to an end—but come to an end it must.

With a heavy heart she made her way towards the sparkling turquoise water. Claudia had taken the children out for the whole day, and Rick was working in his study. She would spend the morning by the pool, and at lunchtime she would broach the subject of their departure.

But as she paused at the entrance of the poolhouse she was startled to see Rick sitting working at an old table, a glass of mineral water at his side, a pile of papers in front of him. He was dressed in frayed denim cut-offs, a faded old T-shirt which made his forearms look spectacularly muscular, and a shabby old straw hat was perched on the dark hair. With his tanned skin and the thick black hair curling on to his neck he looked rakish and piratical, she thought. And dangerously attractive.

He must have heard her, for he looked up briefly, his eyes narrowing as he scanned her.

Something in the way he was looking at her brought the colour to her cheeks. 'I'm sorry—I didn't know you were in here.'

He continued to silently appraise her.

'Stop ogling,' she said crossly, with the kind of unexpectedly easy familiarity produced by weeks of living in close quarters with him. And which was all due to end next week...

'Sorry,' he said, sounding unperturbed and not in the least bit sorry. 'But if you don't want men staring at you, then you really shouldn't walk around in those shorts.'

Her heart had started beating very fast. 'What's wrong with them?'

He smiled at her question, leaning back in his chair, his attention totally on the offending garment. 'Everything. They fit too well at the waist, they cling too much to your bottom. Oh, and they're much too short—all that bare leg is positively indecent.'

It served her right for asking him such a provocative question. 'Rick——'

'I like you not wearing your glasses, too—much less forbidding. Although they can be so much fun to take off, of course. And while we're on the subject,' he murmured, his eyes moving in an upward direction to linger there, 'that T-shirt isn't entirely suitable either—the way it moulds those gorgeous...'

'That's enough!' His words had produced enough goose-bumps to make her teeth want to chatter. 'I came in here to talk to you, not to be——'

'Seduced?' he suggested, with a flash in his eyes.

She swallowed at the seductive devilment she read there. 'Exactly,' she managed primly.

'But oh, Elizabeth,' he sighed. 'Having you around all the time but strictly off-limits is unbearably tantalising, you know.'

'And I suppose you've never had to exercise self-control before,' she observed acidly.

For a second, his eyes became steely. 'You have such a touchingly low opinion of me,' he mocked.

'And whose fault is that?' she shot back.

He sipped at his mineral water. 'Come over here. Sit down.'

'I'll stand, thanks.' She felt safer with as many feet between them as possible.

'What do you want to talk to me about?'

The unthinkable. 'Our flight home.'

'Ah. That's good, Elizabeth—because that's precisely what I want to talk to you about.'

'You do?'

'Uh-huh. You see, I have a proposition to put to you.'

She eyed him suspiciously. 'What kind of proposition?'

'I want you to consider staying here. You and Peter.'

'But that's impossible—Peter starts back at school next week.' She stared at him suspiciously. 'How long did you have in min——?'

'Permanently,' he cut in.

She looked at him. He'd tipped the battered old panama hat over his eyes so that they weren't visible. 'I think you'd better explain what you mean,' she said carefully.

He relented and pushed the hat to the back of his head. 'You've enjoyed yourself here, haven't you? In spite of everything that has happened between us—your stay has been no hardship. Has it?'

He seemed to be waiting for an answer, and Elizabeth was still too stunned by his initial suggestion to be able to utter more than the simple truth. 'No.'

'And Peter——?'

She was in a no-win situation where Peter was concerned. 'Peter loves it here.' She tried not to sound bitter at how he had taken to this bizarre family life like a duck to water. She dreaded what his reaction was going to be when told it was time to go home. 'You know that.'

'Yes,' he echoed quietly. 'I do. As I know that Jessie too is more contented than she's been in a long time.' He looked at her with a piercing stare. 'She likes you,' he said simply. 'Both.'

'And I like her. But I have a life in England—we both do.'

'But you could so easily have a life here, Elizabeth. Your house can be sold—alternatively you might want to let it out. Peter could go to school here—there are some excellent ones nearby.'

She gave a small, wry laugh. 'How disposable you make my life in England sound, Rick. What about my job? I suppose you've considered that?'

He nodded. 'Of course. As you know, I have an organisation big enough to find the perfect job for you.'

She felt as though she were wading through heavy mists. 'And what if I told you that I wouldn't want to work with you?'

That too seemed to have been taken care of. He shrugged. 'I broached the subject with Paul before we left—he's happy to transfer you to one of his branches here in New York.'

'Just a minute!' She stared at him, her eyes wide and incredulous. 'You spoke to Paul? *Before* we left?'

'In passing.'

'In *passing*? You had no right to do that, no right at all. Just what did you tell him?'

'I told him everything,' he said simply. 'About us. I'm fed up with keeping it a secret, as though it's something to be ashamed of.'

'But there *is* no us!' Then she dropped her face into her hand as she imagined the news gathering speed all round the building where she worked. 'Oh, my God,' she said weakly.

'Hear me out,' he persisted. 'Here.' He reached down to the refrigerator, took out two beers and opened them, then handed her a small, frosted bottle.

She took it, grateful enough for something to do with hands which suddenly felt like trembling.

'You don't hate me——'

'Don't lay odds.'

He laughed. 'Or I you. On the contrary, living together has proved remarkably enjoyable, wouldn't you say?'

She would not be drawn. 'And where would we live— Peter and I, that is?'

He looked at her in surprise. 'Why, here, of course. With me. And Jessie.'

There was a tiny little ache in her stomach, but the sardonic tone of her question meant he would never know about it. 'Living as we have been?' she prompted.

'No,' he responded gruffly. 'Not like that.'

Elizabeth digested this. 'I see. So do I take it that this "living together" would include having—how shall I best put it—carnal knowledge of each other?'

He grinned irrepressibly. 'Yes, please!'

She frowned. 'So—is this really some quaint kind of proposal, Rick?'

He shrugged. 'That's up to you. I would prefer to legalise matters, yes—for Peter's sake, if nothing else.'

Her mouth deliberately tightened into an angry line which hid the vulnerable tremor she could feel hovering. How cold he made it sound. Legalise matters, indeed! 'Don't worry!' she returned with fire, her eyes damning him for his insouciance. 'I wouldn't *dream* of putting you through such awful hardship that you'd have to actually *marry* me!'

He gave a slow, lazy smile. 'Oh, it would be no hardship, Elizabeth, I can assure you. No hardship at all. I can't ever remember wanting a woman as much as I want you.'

'There's more to living together than sex,' she snapped, until she saw his small smile, and realised that the way she'd worded her objection meant that he now knew she was giving his suggestion serious thought.

'I agree. But we seem compatible in most other ways too, wouldn't you say? Quite strikingly so.'

'How long have you been thinking along these lines?' she asked suddenly.

He took a long mouthful of beer. 'For some time,' he answered obscurely.

'So I was right about your parents, was I? Have I been staying here on approval? I've made the grade and this is the passing-out parade?'

'It isn't a job,' he reminded her. 'What exactly are your objections?'

'How about trust, Rick? That's number one on my list. How do I know where you'll be spending your nights?'

'Why, I'll be spending them with you, Elizabeth. Exclusively.'

'I advise you not to make a promise you can't keep,' she said, bitterly. 'Did you tell Brooke that, too? Did you promise to be faithful to her, only to leap into bed with the first woman you saw? Or perhaps I *wasn't* the first woman—maybe I was just one in a long, long line——'

'That's enough!' he snarled, slamming his beer bottle down on the table.

'No—it is not enough!' She had religiously put Brooke to the back of her mind for weeks, but now the memory scorched back like a forest fire. 'Tell me about Brooke, Rick. Did you think of her while you lay in bed making love to me? Did you close your eyes and——?'

'*No!*' He made a low, savage noise at the back of his throat, pushing his chair back so violently that it over-turned, his face dark with thunderous rage as he moved towards her.

'No,' she pleaded softly, backing against the wall, but her heart was racing and it was nothing to do with fear. 'I didn't mean it...'

'Oh, yes, you did,' he ground out. 'Just as much as I mean *this*...' and his mouth covered hers.

As soon as he kissed her, she knew she didn't stand a hope in hell of escaping. He was too angry, too aroused, and so was she.

His mouth smothered hers with fierce passion, and his hand moved roughly beneath her T-shirt to cup her breast with exquisite pressure.

'Oh, yes,' he mouthed into her mouth, and she closed her eyes with dizzy pleasure as she felt their tongues collide.

He tore his mouth from hers to lower his head, impatiently moving the T-shirt up so that it lay in folds above the tight thrusting of her breasts in the scarlet satin bikini top.

She heard him groan as she let him unzip her shorts, so that they dropped to the ground, and then his tongue trailed a path down her torso, and he sank to his knees as he found her navel, probed her there gently and wetly; it was a poignant reminder of his child which had grown inside her, and she clutched her hands around his dark head, her hips moving desperately against his broad shoulders. He clasped her bottom and pulled her even closer, burying his face in the softness of her belly and gave a low moan of desire. The sound stirred her senses into a wildness which made her physically weak. Her knees went from beneath her, but his arms caught her as she slid to the floor, bringing her up against his chest, looking down at her as she leant helplessly against him and muttering something beneath his breath.

Impatiently he kicked the overturned chair aside, flung the panama to the opposite side of the room like a discus, and dimly she realised that he was clearing a space for them in the middle of the floor.

'Here?' she questioned weakly.

'Here,' he agreed grimly, but then he gave a strange smile. 'If we wait until I've carried you up to bed, you'll probably have changed your mind.'

Oh, no, she thought, her eyelids fluttering closed as the pleasure began again. Not now, it's much too late. I have to have him...

He pulled the T-shirt from over his head in one easy, fluid movement and her fingers trembled out to trace butterfly kisses on the steely taut wall of his chest, curling small whorls of the thick hair around her index finger, as if she were performing some pagan rite of homage.

'Dreamy witch,' he murmured, uncannily echoing her thoughts as he gently removed her T-shirt and then unfastened her bikini top, the palms of his hands circling round each tumid breast until she moved her hips as pleasure escalated out of control.

His denim cut-offs were removed gingerly, as if he were in extreme discomfort, and she watched with intense excitement as she saw that under them he wore no briefs...not a thing...

'Oh.' It sounded more like a miaou than the tiny sound of breathless expectation which the sight of him, fully naked and fully aroused, caused her to make.

He laughed. 'Now see what a disadvantage you have me at. Me wearing nothing, while you're all covered up with these——' His middle finger went down to lightly brush over the tiny bikini bottoms, his eyebrows rising with frank pleasure as he encountered the moist heat which seared through them, before he slowly took them off and tossed them away so that they landed on top of his hat.

He moved on top of her, kissed the end of her nose. She felt the hard weight of him pushing against her belly, heard the thundering of his heart against her breast, saw his rueful smile. 'This is all going to be over much too quickly, I'm afraid, my darling...'

But she was ready for him, ready for his exquisite capture, at once so strange and yet so instantly familiar. Ready to relearn that primitive rhythm with him. Ready for the strength of his movements as each thrust made his possession more and more complete, propelled her further and further towards delicious release. She felt it building and building relentlessly, and as the first powerful wrench of her womb heralded the perfect spasms of fulfilment she heard him mutter something— her name, she thought—before she felt his own movements pulsating inside her, and his head fell against her neck, his lips just touching the skin there.

Deliberately she made her mind retreat, concentrating only on the closeness of their enwrapped limbs, the tangle of his damp hair in her fingers, the sheen of sweat on his broad brown back. As he gently throbbed into stillness within her, she heard his breathing steady. He raised his head to look down at her flushed cheeks and gave a look that was almost sad.

'Does that make you think any more about staying?'

She could have wept. She pushed hard and ineffectually at his chest, but he withdrew from her immediately. It took an effort for her to speak. 'Damn you, Rick. Was that you just being your persuasive best?'

His face remained impassive. 'It started out in anger, but once it started—I thought that it might tip the scales in my favour, yes. Or are you telling me you didn't enjoy it?'

'You know I did,' she said flatly, sitting up to look around the hut for her discarded clothes. 'But that's not the point!'

He grimaced. 'You're going to do wonders for my ego, do you know that?'

'I'm very sorry if your ego's suffered—I'd hate to do that——'

But he grabbed her bare shoulders, his eyes angry, but she pulled away from him. 'Beth! This could be so good—for all of us. So why the hell are you going all cold on me?'

'Why do you *think*?' she shouted back. 'Because we still haven't resolved anything. We've just had good sex, that's all—and you probably think you've manipulated me into staying. Well, you're *wrong*! I don't want to live my life wondering whose bed you're in whenever you take trips abroad! Maybe Brooke could live with it— but I couldn't.'

There was a long pause and then, without a word, he reached out and pulled on his own denim cut-offs, slipped his feet into the scuffed canvas shoes and stood up, holding out his hand to pull her to her feet. 'Go back to the house and change,' he said abruptly. 'I'm going out.'

Something in the harsh set of his features frightened and confused her. 'Where are you going?'

His voice was grim. 'To do something which I should have done a long time ago. Don't do a thing until I get back—not a thing, do you understand, Elizabeth? We're going to resolve this once and for all.'

Something in his tone froze her to stone, and she sat and watched as he picked up his T-shirt and walked out of the pool-house without another word.

Elizabeth put her crumpled clothes back on then slowly went back to the house, showered, and changed into jeans and a shirt in a deep violet which somehow reflected her mood, her mind still numb and her body still aching from the intensity of their lovemaking and the bitterness of the words they had spoken immediately afterwards. She was now in deeper than ever, his possession of her binding her to him as surely as if he had imprisoned her and thrown away the key. He had made love to her then left her, she thought with bitter sadness as she remembered that angry, set look on his face as he'd walked out of the pool-house.

She was unable to settle to anything. She had no appetite for food. Instead, she wandered aimlessly around the house, like a ghost haunting a place where it had once been happy, lightly running her long fingertips over the surfaces of exquisite furniture as though mentally saying farewell to it all.

The minutes seemed to trickle by, and she was just half-heartedly deciding to make herself a cup of coffee when there was a ring on the doorbell.

She went into the hall and pulled the door open to find herself staring blankly into a face which it took a moment or two to recognise. The same face which had studied her with such pity all those years ago was staring at her coldly now. Rick's aunt.

She was dressed in a linen suit of palest apricot, her hair a perfect sheening cap of white-gold. The face was perfectly made up, the pink polished nails like tiny talons.

She must be, Elizabeth judged, in her early to middle fifties—but she looked at least a decade younger.

And suddenly the missing piece of the puzzle snapped into place.

She stared steadily into ice-blue eyes so like Jessie's, that nagging familiarity she'd always recognised now explained, for Jessie's small, perfect features were the image of this woman's.

'You're Brooke's mother?' she asked slowly.

'I am. I'm Grace Sparden.'

Grace. Yes, it suited her.

'I think it's time you and I had a little talk, don't you—Beth, isn't it?'

Elizabeth felt her knees weaken as she remembered herself at eighteen, appealing to speak to Rick. 'I can't think that we have anything to say to each other.'

'I think I can be of help to you, my dear. Stop you making a fool of yourself.'

Elizabeth swallowed, her confidence fleeing with each word, regressing to become that insecure eighteen-year-old again. 'You'd better come through into the study,' she said quickly, leading the way, feeling like a condemned man on his way to the gallows.

In the study, neither woman sat down. Elizabeth laced her fingers together in front of her to stop them from shaking.

'You said you had something to say to me?'

The older woman gave a cold smile. 'Rick's just been to see me.'

'Has he?' asked Elizabeth, her mind racing.

'Said that you're moving in here with him.'

'I was thinking about it.'

'*Was*?' said Grace sharply.

'Not that I think it has anything to do with you.'

Grace fished around in the white leather bag, took out a long cigarette, and lit it. 'You remember when you came looking for Rick?'

'How am I likely to forget that? You lied to me—you said you were Rick's aunt.'

A cold smile. 'But that's where you're wrong—that's who *you* thought I was. I merely let you carry on believing that.' With frosted lips she pulled heavily on the cigarette. 'Tell me, Elizabeth—what would you do if I told you that he was there? In the flat. With me.'

Elizabeth felt the colour drain from her cheeks. 'I don't believe you.'

Grace gave a nasty laugh. 'You don't think he's capable of it—a man who could deceive his fiancée like that—someone who could get two women pregnant? It's true. He heard the doorbell and hid in the bedroom. I was under strict instructions that if it was you I was to—let me see, now, how did he put it? Oh, yes,' she smiled. '"Get rid of her." That was it. But I knew what he wanted anyway. I might have been his future mother-in-law—but we always had such a *superb* rapport—if you know what I mean...'

Her eyes gleamed with provocation and Elizabeth felt her skin begin to chill, but she turned a proud, stony face towards the other woman. 'Why are you telling me all this?'

Grace shrugged. 'Maybe I feel sorry for you. Rick really *loved* Brooke, but still he cheated on her. He's that kind of man; he'll never change. Some men don't.'

She gave a sly smile. 'He hasn't come back after seeing me, has he? Where is he now?'

'I don't know——'

'And you never *will*. I saw how it was with Brooke. Every time he used to go out, she would sit waiting and thinking, Has he found someone? Who is he with tonight?'

'Get out,' said Elizabeth, in a quiet, shaking voice. 'Take your filthy accusations with you and get out of here right now.'

'But you'll never know, will you?' She stubbed out her cigarette viciously. 'You'll never be able to trust him!'

Dimly Elizabeth heard her leave, her feet slowly taking her up to her own room. She looked around it, like a person whose memory loss had suddenly cleared.

Just what *was* she doing here? Considering tying herself down to a man who would never love her, who was haunted by a vision of the wife he had cheated on— so much so that he couldn't bring himself to mention her name?

I'm not staying, she thought. I can't stay here. I love him too much to ever settle for second best.

She wasn't aware of time passing. She fished her suitcase down from the cupboard and placed it on the bed, and started laying her shoes on the bottom methodically.

'Planning on going somewhere?' came a low drawl from the doorway, and there stood Rick, the sun behind him, making him seem bigger, darker, taller than usual. His massive frame was very still as he watched her jerky movements.

She couldn't look at him. If she looked at him, she might weaken, and she was going to be strong; so strong. 'I'm packing my case, because I think it's time that Peter and I were leaving.'

He didn't move an inch. 'Oh? And were you planning to say goodbye?'

'Of course I was.' And then her dignified resolve broke and she glowered at him. 'Your mother-in-law came round to see me,' she accused.

He moved into the room. 'Ex-mother-in-law,' he corrected coolly. 'Yes, I wondered whether she might.'

The casual query was an affront. 'You *knew* she was coming here?'

'Call it an informed guess.'

'How? Because you're both so *in tune* with each other—as she implied.'

'Come and sit down,' he said gently, walking over to sit on the bed and patting the space beside him. 'I want to talk to you.'

'I don't want to listen to you—I want to go home.' She remained mutinously where she was, her arms folded across her chest, as if by doing that she could protect her heart from being broken.

'Let me tell you a story, Beth.' His gaze was very steady, and he waited until he had her full attention. 'Imagine a young American guy at the beginning of his career who, one summer, took a trip to Europe. He has a girlfriend back at home—a girl from a similar background he met at college. He's not ecstatic, but he's contented. They've drifted along for a year or two, and everyone assumes they'll get married. So the last thing this man is looking for is involvement. He visits France,

Italy, Germany—and then, on his last weekend in London, he meets a girl.'

'Don't——'

He shook his head to silence her. 'He meets a girl,' he continued, 'who makes him realise what's been missing from his life. But the timing is all wrong. He knows what he should do—he should go back to the States and tell his girlfriend it's all over before getting involved. But——' and here he gave a sad, wry smile '—you were impossible to resist, Beth. And I just couldn't walk away from you.'

How could he have done? thought Elizabeth, a pang of guilt hammering through her as she remembered his reluctance to take things further, and her subtle insistence that he do.

The blue-green eyes were very bright. 'So they spend a weekend together—which is almost perfect, but for the guilt he feels. In the middle of the last night he wakes up and looks down at the beautiful girl lying asleep in his arms.' His voice went very quiet as he re-lived what had happened. 'I walked out on to the balcony and knew what I had to do. I had to tell you the truth, Beth—to go back to the States to sort things out and return to you with a clean slate, to start our future. But when I came back into the bedroom——' and a bleak look momentarily darkened his features '—you were gone.'

'I told you—Brooke rang. I felt ashamed, and angry.'

'I know you did. Let me tell you what happened next. I flew back to the States that same morning, told Brooke all about you—and, six weeks later—at the first opportunity I had—I came back to England to look for you.'

She stared at him, her eyes wide behind her glasses. 'But you never found me.'

'Sure I did. I hired a detective. But I was too late,' he said grimly. 'I traced you to a house in Kensington. I remember standing in the rain, staring up at this vast white building, and then you came out. There was a long black car waiting for you. You were wearing black, with pearls at your throat and your ears. I remember thinking that you looked even more beautiful—and then I saw the older guy following you down, and in that moment I hated you. I flew home again, but I just couldn't get you out of my mind. And then I came to my senses. Go and get her, I thought. Fight for her. I had an investigator find out if you were still living in the same place, but by then it was too late—I discovered that you'd married. I thought you must really have been in love to have done that. And I'd lost you.'

Elizabeth blinked. 'So you went back and married Brooke?'

He nodded. 'Except that it wasn't quite that simple. Brooke told me that she was pregnant. I knew that the baby couldn't possibly be mine, because my affair with Brooke had ended the moment I laid eyes on you. She was hysterical. She didn't want to be a single mother. She wanted marriage and nothing else would do. She began to make all kinds of... threats. I feared for the child, and besides, I was pretty low myself. I discovered that I'd lost you, but Brooke and I had always got along—so maybe marriage *was* the answer. For the child's sake, if for nothing else. I wasn't really thinking straight at all...'

Elizabeth flinched. 'So you did the honourable thing and married her, and you all lived happily ever after.'

He gave her a strange look. 'No, Elizabeth. We did not. It was not a marriage as marriage should be. Living with Brooke meant I learnt a lot about her. That she liked variety—particularly in men.' He gave an empty little laugh. 'And as a mother she was little short of terrible. Poor Jessie.' He sighed. 'I did my best to make it up for her as best I could.'

'You have,' she said softly. 'You know you have.'

He gave a small smile. 'Thank you for that.'

'Does Jessie—know?' probed Elizabeth gently. 'That you aren't her real father?'

He shook his head. 'Nope. There isn't really any way to tell a child that her father could have been one of a number of men, and anyway, as far as I'm concerned, she *is* my daughter—now.'

'Oh, God——' Elizabeth bit her lip.

'No one knew bar Brooke, me and Grace. Grace was beside herself when Brooke—her only child—was killed. She made me promise never to sully her dead daughter's reputation, or to reveal the truth about Jessie's parentage. I agreed, I gave her my word—because, somehow I never imagined being close enough to anyone ever again to warrant my telling them. But that was before I found you again, and I realised that if I wanted you to stay here, if Brooke wasn't going to cast a shadow over the rest of our lives, you would have to know, too. That's what I went to tell Grace this morning, as a matter of honour. That I was going to have to break my word, and why. She hit the roof, went crazy...' His blue-green eyes pierced her with their intensity. 'You must have seen how she was——'

Elizabeth nodded. 'I met her before, you know—at your uncle's flat, a few weeks after our affair.'

Lines of tension became etched on his forehead. 'Why did you never tell me before?'

'Because it was something I preferred to forget—what I would call the lowest point of my life. You see, I tried to find you—to tell you about the baby. I thought you had the right to know. Grace came to the door—I thought she was your aunt, and she carried on letting me think that. She told me that you'd gone back to your fiancée. Today she told me that you'd given her instructions to get rid of me, that you were actually hiding from me . . . As well as implying that when you failed to come home this afternoon you were probably sampling the delights of someone else's bed . . .'

His face had gone a kind of grey colour and he swore softly and explicitly beneath his breath. 'There was an emergency on at one of the offices—today of all days. But you, of course, believed her?'

Elizabeth sighed. How much easier if she had. She shook her head. 'Strangely enough, no. I didn't. Over the last few weeks, I've grown to know you properly. It's shallow people who have a need to be promiscuous, and you aren't a shallow man, not by any stretch of the imagination. And I've come to realise that I can't blame you solely for what happened that weekend, either—I wanted you just as much as you wanted me, and I made that clear . . .'

'I should have told you——'

She smiled, gently. 'Yes, you should. But I can see exactly why you didn't.'

He moved across the room to face her, his hand reaching out to hold one of hers, so strong, and warm and comforting. 'Stay with me, Beth.'

She thought how easy it would be, how much she wanted it—but it simply wasn't enough. 'I can't, Rick. Don't you see—this changes nothing?'

His eyes narrowed. 'That my explanation about Brooke counts for nothing?'

'It isn't that...'

'What, then?'

She bit her lip, knowing that only if she told the truth could she ever leave his house with a clear conscience. She lifted her head. 'You can have access to Peter, I promise you that—but I'm not part of the deal.'

'Because...?' His voice sounded dangerously soft.

'Because I've worked hard to get where I am for *me*. It's been a struggle sometimes, but I've never compromised my ideals, not once. I couldn't live with you, wondering whether you might find someone you really cared about. You married Brooke out of a sense of duty, but I don't want you to do the same with me. I can't stay with you, Rick, because I value myself too much and I'm afraid that I couldn't spend my life with a man who didn't love me——'

'Is that what you think?'

She nodded, too emotionally fraught to trust her reply to words.

'Then in that case, my dearest Beth—you really mustn't go... Because you'll never find another man

who loves you as much as I do.' He took her other hand
in his and she looked up at him in bewilderment.

'Yes,' he whispered. 'Love—true and strong and en-
during. For God's sake, Elizabeth, what do you think
I've been trying to tell you? I *love* you—as I have loved
you,' he continued, 'since the first moment I set eyes on
you at that party. I was intrigued by this smart girl who
answered back and was about to walk out of the door!
Through all the years we were apart, I never stopped
loving you. Even when, extraordinarily, I failed to recognise you, there was something about you which tran-
scended even that, something in you reached out to me,
so that I found myself wanting to make love to you with
a fervour which astonished me. I can remember aching
with the need to kiss you in that damned lift, with you
looking down your nose at me.

'And even while I was burning up with jealousy,
thinking that you'd married John for his money—even
that didn't stop me loving you at the same time.

'When I discovered we had a son, I was shocked, yes,
and furious at first, until I realised that here I had the
means to bring us together. And I discovered that we
were as compatible as we'd always been; it was almost
uncanny how I could seem to almost read your mind,
and you mine.'

Elizabeth closed her eyes, then opened them quickly,
afraid that she might wake to find that it had all been
a dream, but one glance at the look of ardour on the
face of the man in front of her told her that all her wishes
had come true. 'Rick——' she whispered.

'No.' He shook his head. 'Let me finish. I want to
live with you, Elizabeth, and to marry you, not because

of Peter, or the fact that Jessie has blossomed under your tender care, but because you are my woman, my soulmate, whom I respect and adore. But——' and here he looked at her sternly '—like you, I have my conditions—and I too couldn't tolerate living with a woman who didn't love me...'

She gave a slow but brilliant smile as she wrapped her arms about his neck. 'Oh, Rick,' she whispered. 'Darling, darling Rick...'

'Do you?'

'What do you think?'

'Then tell me,' he said urgently. 'I need to know.'

'I love you, Riccardo,' she said. 'So very much.'

A look of utter delight softened the harshly handsome features of his face as he lifted her hand to his lips. 'I think that the children might be *almost* as thrilled as I am to hear our news. Which reminds me.' His voice became stern, authoritative, masterful. 'There will be no repeat of the ugly scene you were forced to endure earlier, and Grace's only involvement in our lives will be in her role as Jessie's grandmother. Happy with that?'

Breathlessly, her head resting on his shoulder, all warm and glowing with disbelieving elation, Elizabeth nodded. 'Yes, darling,' she whispered.

He kissed her properly then, and, with a gentleness which thrilled her, he reached down to remove her glasses, kissing the tip of her nose as he did so. Ridiculously, the curious intimacy of this gesture made her want to weep.

'You weren't wearing these the night of the party.'

'Well, you know that old saying about "men never make passes at girls who wear glasses".'

'Rubbish,' he whispered softly. 'I'd make a pass at you whatever you wore. Is that why you left them off that night?'

'Actually, Donna—the girl I was staying with—insisted I didn't wear them. The only trouble was that I couldn't really see properly without them—you were only a blur until you came up close.'

'Which explains why you looked right through me—it gave me quite a shock. Nothing like *that* had ever happened to me before!'

'Then your ego jolly well *needed* puncturing!' she retorted, but he was laughing.

'Witch!' he chuckled as he moved her a little closer, but she pulled back.

'There's something you should know too,' she said quietly. 'That when I met John he was already a very sick man. I was pregnant and alone, and he was . . . just alone, really. We married for companionship and security—but emotional security, not material. But that's all we ever were—companions——'

He put his finger over her lips. 'Darling, darling—you don't have to. Don't say any more.'

'What—what I'm trying to tell you is that you were my only lover,' she whispered. '*Are* my only lover.'

He pulled her into the warm haven of his chest and began to unbutton her shirt. 'It's a good thing we shan't be disturbed for several hours,' he remarked. 'Because do you have any idea what I'm going to do to you right now?'

'Absolutely no idea whatsoever,' she said innocently. 'Perhaps you'd better tell me?'

And, bending his head to her ear, he proceeded to do exactly that!

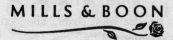

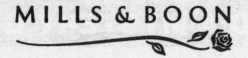

MILLS & BOON

Next Month's Romances

Each month you can choose from a wide variety of romance with Mills & Boon. Below are the new titles to look out for next month.

THE SHINING OF LOVE	Emma Darcy
A BRIEF ENCOUNTER	Catherine George
SECRET OBSESSION	Charlotte Lamb
A VERY SECRET AFFAIR	Miranda Lee
DEAREST LOVE	Betty Neels
THE WEDDING EFFECT	Sophie Weston
UNWELCOME INVADER	Angela Devine
UNTOUCHED	Sandra Field
THIEF OF HEARTS	Natalie Fox
FIRE AND SPICE	Karen van der Zee
JUNGLE FEVER	Jennifer Taylor
BEYOND ALL REASON	Cathy Williams
FOREVER ISN'T LONG ENOUGH	Val Daniels
TRIUMPH OF LOVE	Barbara McMahon
IRRESISTIBLE ATTRACTION	Alison Kelly
FREE TO LOVE	Alison York

GET 4 BOOKS
AND A MYSTERY GIFT

FREE

Return the coupon below and we'll send you 4 Mills & Boon romances absolutely FREE! We'll even pay the postage and packing for you.

We're making you this offer to introduce you to the benefits of Reader Service: FREE home delivery of brand-new Mills & Boon romances, at least a month before they are available in the shops, FREE gifts and a monthly Newsletter packed with information.

Accepting these FREE books places you under no obligation to buy, you may cancel at any time, even after receiving just your free shipment. Simply complete the coupon below and send it to:

HARLEQUIN MILLS & BOON, **FREEPOST**, PO BOX 70, CROYDON CR9 9EL. ✂

- -

Yes, please send me 4 Mills & Boon romances and a mystery gift as explained above. Please also reserve a subscription for me. If I decide to subscribe I shall receive 6 superb new titles every month for just £11.40* postage and packing free. I understand that I am under no obligation whatsoever. I may cancel or suspend my subscription at any time simply by writing to you, but the free books and gift will be mine to keep in any case. *I am over 18 years of age.*

NO STAMP NEEDED

1EP5R

Ms/Mrs/Miss/Mr _____

Address _____

_____

_____

_____ Postcode _____

mps MAILING PREFERENCE SERVICE

DMA

Temptation

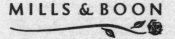

Lost Loves

'Right Man...Wrong time'

All women are haunted by a lost love—a disastrous first romance, a brief affair, a marriage that failed.

A second chance with him...could change everything.

Lost Loves, a powerful, sizzling mini-series from Temptation continues in April 1995 with...

**Even Cowboys Get the Blues
by Carin Rafferty**

MILLS & BOON